What

What is Invisible

What is Invisible

stories by
Beth Ryan

killick press
an imprint of Creative Publishers

St. John's, Newfoundland and Labrador
2003

Le Conseil des Arts | The Canada Council
du Canada | for the Arts

We acknowledge the support of The Canada Council for the Arts for our
publishing program.

We acknowledge the financial support of the Government of Canada through the
Book Publishing Industry Development Program (BPIDP) for our
publishing program.

∞ Printed on acid-free paper

Cover art by Justin Hall
*Earlier versions of several of these stories have been published or broadcast before. They
include: Light Fingers (TickleAce and CBC Radio), Touching Down (CBC Radio), and
Family Business (Hearts Larry Broke).*

Published by
KILLICK PRESS
an imprint of CREATIVE BOOK PUBLISHING
a division of Creative Printers and Publishers Limited
a Print Atlantic associated company
P.O. Box 8660, St. John's, Newfoundland and Labrador A1B 3T7

First Edition
Typeset in 12 point Goudy Old Style

Printed in Canada by:
PRINT ATLANTIC

National Library of Canada Cataloguing in Publication

Ryan, Beth
        What is invisible : stories / by Beth Ryan.

ISBN 1-894294-61-0

        I. Title.

PS8585.Y33W44 2003   C813'.6   C2003-904495-5

For my parents

Bill Ryan (1939-2000)
and
Anne Kieley Ryan

for showing me the value of
a good story well-told

Contents

It is only through the heart that one can see rightly;
what is essential is invisible to the eye.

Antoine de Saint-Exupéry

Northern Lights

They could have been in the Legion back home for all anyone could tell. A two-piece band from Placentia is playing – one guy on electric guitar and the other on an electronic keyboard that imitates everything from a piano to a full brass band. A team of women is in the kitchen keeping an eye on the pots of pea soup and turkey soup simmering on the industrial-sized stoves. And, like home, everyone in the place is linked by blood or marriage or history with just about everyone else.

Sharon watches the action from behind the bar. She and the other bartenders are on loan this evening from the lounge out on the highway, run by Elsie Bennett, a woman from Corner Brook. Everyone arrives, all nice and proper, their lipstick on and their ties straight. They stamp the snow off their boots in the front porch and shed their winter coats. Sharon knows the routine once they get inside. The men head to the bar first and start with a double shot of rum, which they kick back immediately. The women take their time and case the room, seeing who's there and who's not. But once they get their first drink into them, there's no stopping them, either.

The place is done up with crepe paper and flowers made out of tissue. Four colours, all pastels. Long tables run along the walls, covered in paper tablecloths and trays of food. The women are all decked out in dresses of shiny polyester and other shimmery fabrics, with their hair swept up and lacquered in place with a sticky coat of hair spray. The men are in suits that have just come back from the dry cleaners, some of them a little tight across the shoulders. It doesn't matter though because they'll all have their jackets off before the party gets going.

Across the room, Sharon can see Marie Williams, who's married to the pharmacist and works in the drugstore part time. Sweet as you please when she's behind the cash, but wait until she gets a couple of White Russians into her. She's wearing a frothy pink thing with a bow on the arse.

"Looks like an old bridesmaid's dress," Sharon sniffs.

Then there's Mrs. James, who must be close to eighty. There aren't many old people around Fort McMurray, but she's one who made the trek west to be with her kids and grandchildren. She trundles up to the bar and opens a heavy black pocketbook, roots through it for her coin purse. She drinks scotch and waves away any offers of ice or water.

"Neat," she says. "I like it neat."

Tonight, she is dolled up, too, wearing a brocade dress that could have been made from living room curtains. Sharon checks out her own outfit in the mirrored tiles that are stuck on the walls around the bar. On special occasions like this, she and the other waitresses dress up a little and wear black skirts and white blouses with a ruffle in the front. It was her idea.

"Add a bit a class to the place," she told Elsie, who thought that was a grand plan.

But some of the other girls complained. Marlene started whining as soon as she heard about it.

"Fine for you, Sharon," she hissed. "You got nothing to do all day except iron blouses. But I got youngsters and a husband and housework to do before I come here. And I don't got the time to do any extra load of whites every time I get something spilt over the front of that blouse."

Sharon didn't care. She got herself a new white blouse at the Discount Barn and tucked it into a short black skirt with a wide belt. Standing up on the edge of the bathtub at home, she sized herself up in the mirror on the medicine chest and decided she looked pretty good. When she came downstairs, her brother asked if she was hoping to pick up an old geezer at the party.

"Very funny," she spat at him and left him laughing his head off at the kitchen table.

*****

Walter's aunt is right in the middle of the action tonight. Theresa loves making a fuss, so planning a big do at the community centre is just her speed. The occasion is her best friend's 25th wedding anniversary, but that's just the excuse to get everyone from home together for a party. It's an idea that Walter has had trouble getting used to since he arrived last spring. People who you barely spoke to back home become your best pals when you're living thousands of miles from home.

Some of the guys Walter went to school with are on the same shift with him at Syncrude. They joke around with him and reminisce about good times back in high school.

"Remember that, Wally?" one of them will say, cuffing him on the arm in a show of camaraderie.

But Walter does not remember. He was not along for that weekend at the cabin or that beach party. He had only one friend in high school, and David is not among the crew here in Fort McMurray. David went on to university at St. Francis

Xavier in Nova Scotia and works for the feds in Ottawa these days.

Walter shrugs off invitations to go for a beer with the guys at the end of their shift. He's much happier to come home from work each evening and play with his young cousins for a while before supper. They run him ragged with horsey rides on his shoulders and mad wrestling matches on the living room carpet. After supper, he retreats to the basement to spend a few hours on his latest woodworking project. Using a set of tools he received as a birthday gift two years ago, Walter creates wooden decorations for the front lawn for Christmas, Hallowe'en and any other occasion that catches his Aunt Theresa's attention. A sleigh for Santa pulled by eight reindeer. Little elves painted with red and green suits. Witches riding brooms. Pumpkins with toothy grins. The decorations are always the talk of the town. Families file by in their cars or on foot as soon as Walter turns the lights on for the first time each year. At Christmas, the kids are beside themselves, stumbling through the yard in their bulky snowsuits and boots, exclaiming at each new decoration.

He was in the basement painting the leaves of a St. Patrick's Day shamrock when Theresa called downstairs to say it was almost time to go.

"Come on, good looking!" she beckoned him. "Get up here and put on your nicest shirt for the big party!"

Theresa is his mother's youngest sister – only four years older than him. Walter had trained as a welder back home, going to the Trades College and getting his papers. He could have landed a good job in St. John's, but Theresa called from Fort McMurray to say they were looking for welders at Syncrude, with a salary he had never even dreamed of making in his life. His mother paid for the plane ticket, and he arrived in Alberta three weeks later.

"Okay," he called up the stairs. "I'll be ready in five minutes."

If it wasn't for Theresa, Walter would not be going to this damn party.

*****

Sharon was only a kid of 11 or 12 when Walter was found in a snowbank behind the school, nearly dead from exposure. But she remembers the exact look on her mother's face when she heard the news from her sister. She stood by the phone, the receiver pressed into her chest and one hand over her mouth. When she hung up the phone, she turned towards the stairway and called to Sharon's older brother.

"Dan, get downstairs right now," she said, and it only took him a few seconds to make his way to the kitchen.

"What's going on?" he asked, trying for nonchalance.

"What do you know about what happened to Walter Norman last night?" his mother asked.

Sharon had never seen her brother looked scared before. This was entertaining.

"Look, Mom, I had nothing to do with it," he said. "I was there with the boys, but I cleared out before they got into anything."

The story came out in pieces over a couple of days. A bunch of guys had convinced Walter to come with them for a booze-up behind the store, which was strange in itself. Walter never ran with a crowd, let alone the coolest guys in town. Next thing, they were pouring swish down his throat, the hard liquor that comes from filling empty rum barrels with water and letting the rum seep out of the wood.

Someone started pushing him, and another guy gave him a few belts to the stomach. Soon, everyone was getting in a smack or a kick at Walter. In the end, his coat was hauled off his back and he was tossed in the snowbank "to sober up," one of them snickered.

"I am so ashamed. I can't look at you," Sharon's mother told Dan. "What did that poor youngster ever do to you?"

She was the only one to speak up in Walter's defense. The adults claimed he just got himself into some good old-fashioned trouble, out drinking with the boys. The guys who were there that night were pissed off when they heard that Walter was found in the snowbank by the RCMP a few hours later. Had to go and call attention to himself, didn't he? The rest of the kids just steered clear of him. He might have been kind of a quiet loser before, but now he had the stamp of "victim" on his forehead. No one wanted that to taint them.

Walter came back to school a few days later, faded bruises still visible on his face. He barely said a word for the rest of year, and everyone went back to ignoring him. In the months that followed, the guys who had led the attack on Walter hit a stretch of bad luck. A boulder the size of a soccer ball made its way through the windshield of Harry Collier's Trans-Am when it was parked outside the Legion on a Friday night. A mysterious fire nearly burnt down a little cabin outside of town where the boys hung out on weekends. Darren Janes tripped in a rabbit snare that turned up outside his back door and wound up with blackened eyes and a broken nose from the fall. Sharon was secretly gleeful each time she heard the news. What goes around comes around, she figured.

*****

The dancing is underway early tonight. Usually, everyone needs a few drinks to get going. But a couple of women got up by themselves and put on a fine show in the middle of the floor, swaying to the music in their too-tight jeans and high-heel shoes. It wasn't long before a few of the guys got in on the action, whisking the girls away to be their own dance partners.

Walter crouches in the corner on one of the stiff plastic chairs, his elbows resting on his knees. He holds a beer by its neck, his fourth already this evening, taking a swig whenever someone looks in his direction. Whenever he can, he snatches a look at Debbie Connors. She went to Trades School the same time that he did. She showed up in Fort McMurray before Christmas after some trouble at home. Everyone was buzzing about it, but Walter never bothered to get the details. He knows that half the stories are never true.

Debbie's a good-looking girl, with her silky brown hair and big green eyes. Her eyebrows are tweezed in a dramatic arch, a style that makes her look as if she's always amazed. She knows all too well that she makes the men silly and useless. She has been at the centre of many a fight at the local bar, watching with a smirk as a couple of guys pound each other senseless in a battle for her affection. She is in the middle of a story, her hands fluttering dramatically in the air, the people around her laughing. She turns slightly to the left and catches Walter in mid-stare. She promptly sashays across the room, a little drunk but still her brazen self.

"I hear somebody just had hisself a birthday," she says, leaning into his face, her breath hot with the smell of dark rum.

Walter leans back in his chair, moving away from Debbie as fast as he can. He knows what will happen next. If he speaks to a stranger or more than a couple of people at a time, Walter's face will turn purple and his throat will close over. His hands will start to shake as if he has been gripped by a seizure. Walter had always been quiet and a bit nervous, and his father mocked him for his reserved nature, often trying to goad him into action. But his mother would not tolerate it.

"Leave him alone, Clyde. He'll grow out of it when he's good and ready!"

Now, after just turning the big 3-0, nothing has changed for Walter. He stares at Debbie Connors as if she is a menacing creature from a low-budget horror flick.

"I didn't give you a birthday kiss," Debbie says, her mouth moving towards his face.

Her lips are shiny with lipstick and her tongue darts between his lips, probing the inside of his mouth. Walter closes his eyes and waits for it to be over. His lips are slack and unresponsive.

"Hey," Debbie says, her face screwed up in confusion.

No one has ever greeted her with such a lack of enthusiasm. She stares at him for a moment and then turns to walk away. Over her shoulder, she hisses at him.

"What are you? Some kind of faggot?"

*****

Sharon watches Debbie descend on Walter from across the room. There is always a Debbie in every town, and if there isn't, they'd probably have to import one. In Sharon's hometown, the girl was Cathy Doyle. One night at a dance, she went out to her car to get her cigarettes and found her fiancé in the back seat with Cathy Doyle. Her mother thought she overreacted to the situation. She still can't get over the idea that Sharon gave back the engagement ring that Eddie Kennedy had given her.

"You're twenty-six years old, my darling. Don't think you're going to get many more chances," she warned her.

"Jesus, Mom, he was in my friggin' car with another woman! What do you expect me to do after that?"

But her mother just shook his head and muttered about forgiveness and men's needs and looking at things in the big picture.

"I see the big picture," Sharon yelled back at her. "Eddie Kennedy is an arsehole and I'm not going to be stuck with him the rest of my lousy life."

Giving back that ring was the most satisfying thing she did all year. She walked up to him in the Seawinds Lounge, pushing through a crowd of guys who were standing around drinking beer, and gave him the fake velvet box with the ring in it. He had asked the store to size the ring especially for her, so he probably wouldn't get his money back. And Cathy Doyle had fingers like blood puddings, so it wouldn't fit her. Eddie just stood there, tongue flapping soundlessly, and looked from her to the boys to the box in his hand, his eyes moving in a slow-motion circle.

When it comes down to it, Sharon figures she should send Cathy a thank-you card. Thank you for having such bad taste in men. Thank you for getting drunk on two bottles of India beer. Thank you for giving me a good excuse to call off the engagement. Sharon was planning to have her wedding reception at the Legion in July. She had paid the manager $100 as a deposit, and that was supposed to be non-refundable. But when she told the guy about the car and the ring and Cathy and Eddie, the old frigger was pretty good about it. His eyes darted around to make sure no one was looking and he pressed a roll of twenty-dollar bills into Sharon's hand.

"Excuse me, ducky, but I'd like another White Russian."

It's Marie Williams, her elbows propped up on the bar, all cutesy and sweet. She's bopping in time to the music, tapping her frosty pink nails on the bar. Sharon splashes the liquor into the glass and tops it up with milk.

"Thanks, darlin'," Marie says, giving Sharon the once-over before she sidles off on her satin pumps.

*****

Walter slips out the front door of the community centre in a desperate attempt to elude Debbie Connors and makes his way to the picnic tables out back. It is blessedly quiet outside, a relief from the music and voices at the party. Walter sweeps a sprinkle of snow from the top of a table and climbs up to have a seat. He is not sure what fuelled Debbie's fleeting interest in him. Women have never given him much attention, unless they are looking for help. Not that Walter really minds. That's how Tammy found him.

Walter was hard at work on Theresa's flower beds one day last summer when a pickup truck pulled up outside the house next door. A couple from Newfoundland was moving into the basement apartment. She looked no more than a teenager, her tiny body swollen by pregnancy. He was a good bit older and hard as nails, as far as Walter could tell. They bickered constantly for the rest of August; the open windows helped to carry the sounds of arguments and slamming doors across the lawn to where Walter stood, listening helplessly.

Then, one morning, it was quiet. The girl sat on the steps, smoking a cigarette and crying. Walter was mowing the back lawn, watching her carefully from under the peak of his baseball cap. When he finished, he went over to the fence separating the two gardens and peered over the top at her.

"You okay?" he asked, squinting into the sun.

She shook her head and bent down to put out her cigarette on the concrete step below.

"He's gone and left me."

Walter waited to see if she'd elaborate, but she folded her arms over her knees and buried her face in them. He stepped around the fence and into her yard.

It turned out that Tammy wasn't a teenager, but she wasn't far off. She was 22 and awfully naive, Walter concluded. He puffed up in her presence and became bigger and stronger than he ever thought he could be. He helped her around the apartment by installing new curtain rods and painting the bedroom. On Saturdays, he drove around Fort McMurray with her, scouting out bargains on cribs and strollers and the myriad of things a little baby apparently needed for its first year of life. Tammy told him about her epileptic seizures and gave him a spare key so he could check on her if he heard some noise or didn't see her around for a while. More than once, Walter sat beside her as she lay on the floor, her body fighting the seizure, her limbs jerking and flailing.

The night her water broke, she called Walter. He ran across the lawn in his bare feet and stubbed his toe on the concrete step on the way in the door. He hopped inside, holding the wounded foot in one hand, and found Tammy sitting on the kitchen floor. She looked up at him and started to cry.

"Don't worry," Walter told her, grabbing the phone.

He called 9-1-1 and sputtered directions into the phone. The operator kept telling him to repeat the address until he yelled it clearly into the mouthpiece. Then he turned his attention to Tammy and grabbed some paper towels to mop up the water around her. By the time the ambulance showed up fifteen minutes later, Walter had helped Tammy into dry clothes and gathered some of her belongings into a small suitcase. He stepped outside while the paramedics tended to Tammy and was ready to go back to his own house when the female paramedic stuck her head out the door.

"Are you Walter?"

He nodded.

"She says she won't go to the hospital unless you come with her."

Less than an hour later, Walter sat in the delivery room and held Tammy's hand as she screamed her way through a series of intense but short-lived labour pains. He watched in amazement as she pushed a five-pound baby into the world. The doctor, assuming he was the father, asked if he'd like to cut the umbilical cord. Tammy, dreamy and dazed from the labour, nodded at him to go ahead. Walter took the scissors offered by the nurse and aimed them at the spot on the cord between two clamps.

"Give it a good, strong snip, Dad," the doctor urged Walter.

It took Walter a couple of attempts – the idea of cutting flesh was unnerving – but when the scissors made a clean cut through the cord, he felt a swell of relief and, inexplicably, pride. He didn't actually do anything to make this baby!

Ever since that night, Walter has been there whenever Tammy needs anything, whether it is pushing the stroller around the block to give her a chance to sleep or driving her and the baby to doctor's appointments. Tammy thanks him every day and tries to show her gratitude by having him over for supper several times a week. This development caught his Aunt Theresa's attention.

"Walt, are you sure you want to get tangled up with that little girl?" she asked, peering over a cup of tea at him one night after supper.

"We're friends, Theresa. It's not a big deal."

"No, my darling, she doesn't want to be your friend," Theresa said, shaking her head.

Walter considered that idea for a moment. It hadn't occurred to him that Tammy had any intentions that weren't completely platonic. But he had to admit that after the baby was settled in her crib for the night, they often sat on the couch together and watched television. Tammy always plunked down close to him, close enough for their shoulders to touch and her hand to graze his thigh when she reached for something on the coffee table. And she had taken to kissing him goodbye when he left her place each evening. A sweet kiss, placed neatly on his mouth. It did not ask to be reciprocated, the kiss; it was just given to him. Those clues had gone unnoticed by Walter until now. The thought of Tammy, her pale, pretty face turned up to his, made him feel overcome, as if he couldn't breathe. He pushed his chair back from the table and carried his plate to the sink.

"I'm just going out for a bit of fresh air," he told Theresa.

*****

Sharon cuts through the kitchen on her way to the back door. She needs a smoke desperately. Outside, she sucks the crisp air into her lungs and hesitates before lighting a cigarette. The colours are intense tonight. Waves of green, pink, red and yellow shimmer against the black sky. Aurora Borealis. Sharon remembers this from her Grade Five literature book. She did a project about the Northern Lights, with help from her father. He told her stories about seeing the colours flickering in the night sky over Fogo Island when he was a boy.

"We'd get out of our beds to see the lights! You haven't seen anything like it, my dear. Way better than the fireworks we have now," he told her.

Sharon takes out her lighter and leans towards her cigarette. In the glow of the flame she can see the outline of a body sitting on the picnic table, shoulders rounded and head down. It's Walter. He has grown up into a solid man, she realizes, broad through the back and quite tall. He is not the sad, straggly teenager she knew back home. She makes her way to him, the snow crunching under her shoes.

"This seat taken?" Sharon pats the table beside him.

Walter turns his head and peers up at her over the sleeve of his coat.

"It's all yours."

He shakes his head at her offer of a cigarette and they sit silently, watching the light show going on above their heads.

"So are you liking it out here, Walter? Being away from home?" Sharon asks after a few minutes has slipped by.

"Not really away, are we?" Walter laughs quietly. "Can't swing a cat around here without hitting someone from home!"

Sharon giggles at the idea of the cat flying through the air, striking Marie Williams in the head with a thud, a sound like a pumpkin smashing into the pavement on Hallowe'en night.

"True enough," she says.

"I s'pose we could try to get further away from home. Vancouver maybe," Walter muses.

"But they'd find us anyway."

"No point in running, I guess," Walter says.

They trade stories of their jobs, the people they have in common, the antics of Debbie Connors. It's the longest conversation Walter and Sharon have ever shared.

"Do you like to have a game of pool?" Sharon asks, after another quiet spell has passed.

"Sure. The odd time I do."

"Well, you should come out to the club some night. I get off early on Wednesdays. We could have a drink and play a few games," Sharon offers.

"Maybe I will."

*****

Walter gets home from the party late and a little drunk. One of the guys from work gives him a ride home, after convincing him to leave his truck in the parking lot for the night. He staggers on the front walkway and laughs to himself. Across the lawn, a light burns in the bathroom window of Tammy's apartment. He wonders if the baby is up. She has been teething lately and crying for hours at night, keeping Tammy from getting a decent sleep. He picks his way over the bumpy snow to the door of the apartment and raps gently on the glass. Tammy's face appears and she squints into the tiny window, trying to figure out who's there. The door swings open and Walter steps inside.

The Lizard's Skin

Three days after Abby's husband left her, her mother calls from St. Petersburg to see how she is holding up. Doris starts out with her soft mommy routine; she babies Abby and makes supportive noises. Then she tries a little pull-up-your-socks speech, designed to antagonize Abby into action. Eventually, Doris tries to convince her to cash in some airline points and get herself a ticket to Florida.

"Come now before all the bloody tourists get here for Christmas," Doris says, with the arrogance of one who's spent four winters in the sun.

"I hate hot weather. You know that," Abby says, and even she is annoyed by the petulance in her voice.

"Then this is the perfect time to come," Doris responds triumphantly. "The temperatures are in the low seventies. No humidity at all! It's very comfortable."

Abby manages to get her mother off the phone by promising to think about it, and then she spends the rest of day on the couch, wrapped in an enormous, puffy comforter. She does nothing but stare at the Weather Channel and analyse the weather trends across the country and down in the States. Doris wasn't lying. The temperatures for St. Pete Beach are very nice. The idea of swimming pools and sandy beaches suddenly becomes quite appealing. Warm water sloshing over her feet as she walks on the heated sand, sunglasses to keep her from looking people in the eye. She rolls off the couch and onto the floor and sits for a moment to assess the pros and cons.

Pros: getting away from everyone's pitying faces, not being at home if Michael decides to call, having a good reason not to go to work.

Cons: fighting off her mother for a couple of weeks.

At the Tampa airport, Abby springs for a real cab instead of the mini-van. It costs fifty bucks American, but she doesn't want to make polite chitchat with the British tourists and the Canadian snowbirds. Instead, she sits silently in the back seat of a cab that sails through the traffic over the bridge into St. Pete Beach.

Doris lives in a condominium, a pink stucco building that forms an "L" around the pool. It looks like a motel from the fifties, with the doors to each unit opening to the outside and swirling iron staircases that lead up from the ground to the second floor. The whole neighbourhood looks as if it was plucked out of the set for an old movie. But then, judging by the average age of the crowd she sees tottering around the pool, Abby figures they're right at home at this 1950s nostalgia party.

On the first day in Florida, Abby wakes up at dawn, confused by the intense sunlight. She retreats under the covers for a few more hours before she gives in to the sun and climbs out of bed. Swimming is a good idea, she decides, a good way to be alone, to get away from Doris and the torrents of advice that pour, unprovoked, from her mouth. Abby puts on her bathing suit and gets ready to go to the pool. But Doris heads her off at the pass, popping out from the kitchenette with a plateful of apple danish.

"Darling, have a little bite to eat before you go out," she coos, thrusting the plate in Abby's face.

"You don't want me to get a cramp and sink to the bottom of the pool, do you?" Abby says, tossing one of Doris' standard warnings back in her face.

Doris screws up her face in disapproval.

"Oh, aren't you the smart one," she snaps back.

She gives Abby a stern look, assessing her bathing suit (a few years old), her legs (white as a boiled potato) and her feet (naked of any bright nail polish).

"Well, you could at least put on a little lipstick," Doris says, as if it's the only lifeline she can extend.

"Thanks. You look gorgeous, too," Abby says, poking though the hall closet for a towel.

Doris is not deterred. She comes out of the bathroom, armed with a silvery pink lipstick. Abby puts some on and dashes out the door. Doris grabs her big, floppy sunhat off a chair and clatters behind Abby in a ridiculous pair of open-toed mules.

"Wait for me," she trills as Abby turns the corner and goes down the stairs.

It is only 8:30 in the morning, but Doris insists on parading her around the pool like Miss Canada in the swimsuit competition. She is dying to introduce her to all the neighbours. Doris steers Abby towards a group that is sitting around one of the patio tables, in the shade of a blue and white umbrella. A pair of couples, about 65 or a little older, with intense suntans and grey hair that's growing yellow from the sun. Stella, Harold, Bernice, Marty. Bernice is serving coffee from a thermal carafe, and when she sees Doris and Abby, she turns to Marty and gives him a coy look.

"Darling, will you run up to the condo and get us a couple of mugs," she says, head turned up to him.

She doesn't need to beg. Marty is on his feet before she even has the sentence out of her mouth. His devotion is sweet and familiar to Abby. It reminds her of Michael – the steady, unabated adoration he showed her early on.

*****

In the first few months of her relationship with Michael, Abby resisted the very thing that drew her to him in the first place. His steadiness, his loyalty, his calm observances of routine and ritual. He would say, "I'll call you around 8 o'clock." The phone would ring at 8:02. And he always sounded so totally delighted to find her there, as if she were an unexpected but pleasant surprise. But after years of yearning for security and commitment, Abby was suddenly longing for the wild days, the unpredictable nature of other boyfriends, the thrill of never knowing if they wanted her and wondering what she could do to entrance them.

Her best friend, Carol, called the first time Michael went away for the weekend without her. He was off on a canoeing trip with a bunch of his friends. They went every October – the same five guys each year.

"Come on," Carol said. "You can't be moping around like you're lost without him. That's not like you."

Which, of course, was true. Abby was not used to having someone to miss, someone to plan her activities around. So Carol and Abby went out for a beer that night and sat at the bar, taking a couple of bar stools away from the regulars. A guy they went to university with ambled in through the door.

"Here he comes." Carol nudged Abby. "God's gift to the environment."

Abby looked up and saw Jamie Piercey trundling across the room, hair in his face, crumpled Army jacket hanging off him. He was tall, skinnier than he was in the old days, and a little mangy-looking. His eyes were glazed and he looked a bit

stunned. He's been smoking too much dope, Abby concluded.

"He used to be so cute! Remember?" Carol hissed. "But,
my gawd, look at him. He's a streel! He's in with some kind
of hippie environmental crowd. You can't even talk to him
anymore."

Jamie saw them and headed for the bar, a big, open smile
on his face.

"Hey there, Carol," he said before turning to Abby. "Now,
you're a stranger!"

He hugged Abby, too tightly and for too long. She inhaled
the stale, sweet smell of his unwashed jacket. Jamie ordered a
beer and hauled up another bar stool.

"So, I hear you've got yourself a new man," Jamie said,
pressing Abby for details. "Where did you meet? What does
he do? What are his five best character traits?"

"He's very sweet," Abby said. "And he's steady, and loyal.
And he's really easy to be around."

"That's only four traits," said Jamie. "But, so far, he
sounds like a Labrador retriever."

"Well, that's your interpretation," she said and turned
back to the bar to order a beer.

"Whatever makes you happy makes me happy," he said,
bright and smiling again.

"Here, I have something for you," he said, and reached
behind his neck to undo the clasp on a gold chain. He lifted
it over his head, catching the chain in his hair, untangled it,
and held it in front of Abby's face. A crucifix, less than an
inch long, hanging from a tiny loop.

"It's for you. I want you to wear it," he said. He took her
hand and curled the chain into her palm, folding her fingers
over it.

"I gotta run. I'll be seeing you," he said, kissing her face just to the left of her mouth.

Michael got home late Sunday night and came in to see her even before he unpacked the car. She met him at the door in her bathrobe.

"Hey you," he said, pulling her to him. Abby's body turned into a straight line, taut and unyielding.

Michael made her a cup of tea and told her about the trip. There are stories about how Greg toppled the canoe and how Brian drank too much at the campsite and started singing Johnny Cash songs. He laughed so hard in the telling that she almost forgot that there was something sad and heavy in her belly. Before they went to bed, he put the chain on the front door and checked the deadbolt on the back door. She went on upstairs and climbed into bed with her bathrobe still pulled tight around her. When he finally leaned over to turn off the light, he saw the gold chain and cross on the bed-side table.

"This is new," he said, running the filmy gold through his fingers.

"No, not really. It belongs to Jamie Piercey."

"What's it doing here?"

She waited for a few seconds, as if she were thinking back, as if she were saying to herself: how did that thing get here?

"He gave it to me," Abby said eventually.

His face was still as he considered this.

"He was here?"

She said nothing. He looked at her, then away, and then back into her face.

"Jesus," he said and climbed out of bed. He stopped at the door and looked back at her.

"Do you want to say something to me?"

"I'm sorry."

He came back into the room to gather his clothes from the chair. He walked out, and this time, he did not look back. She heard him outside the door, struggling into his clothes, and then, his soft, careful steps on the stairs. Finally, he was gone. He didn't slam the door. He used his key to turn the deadbolt.

Abby went out every night for the next two weeks and sat in loud, smoky bars featuring bands with varying degrees of talent. On Saturday night at the Ship Inn, the lights went out as the band launched into the fourth song of their first set.

"It's just as well," she complained to Carol. "I'd have to throw myself into the bloody harbour if he sang another rip-the-guts-out-of-you, love-gone-wrong song."

Carol sucked on her cigarette and waved a dismissive hand in Abby's face.

"Don't come bawling to me about your broken heart! It's your own fault," she said.

The singer strummed his guitar, and all he could hear was the soft twang of an acoustic instrument. The drummer rapped out a *be-dum-ching* rhythm, and everyone laughed.

"I guess I am just the most powerful man in Newfoundland," the singer chuckled and feigned a little aw-shucks kick with the toe of his cowboy boot.

"Go on!" someone yelled in the darkness. "You sucked all the power out of the place."

People chattered, wondering what had happened. The sound guy and bass player checked out the gear and tried to figure out if they had blown the circuits in the bar. The bartender went from table to table, offering little candles. Soon, the singer was helping her, as if this had happened at his house, and he was obliged to make his guests comfortable.

Abby was thinking about her house, just two blocks away. Was the power out there, too? There had been a couple of break-ins on the street. She pictured a grubby-looking teenager on the back step, breaking the window out of the door, slipping his greasy hand inside and turning the knob, letting himself into the kitchen, and then the rest of the house.

"I'm going," she said and turned to Carol.

"What? And miss all the excitement? Someone is going to try to rob a purse or at least grope someone while the lights are out," she said.

Duckworth Street was black. Abby waded through the darkness, making her way along the sidewalk, clinging to the storefronts. Cars glided by and splashed light in her path. When she turned the corner and climbed the hill, she could barely pick her house out of the murky shadows. Her heart pulsed in her throat as she turned the key in the deadbolt. She stepped into the front hallway and stood still. All she could hear was the soft whoosh of car tires on the street.

Abby found a candle in the living room and groped through the kitchen drawer for the big box of matches that Michael had put there for that very purpose. He thought of everything. She struck a match, watching the flame sizzle and spring to life. She lit a candle and moved it near the phone. She waited for a few minutes, and then she picked it up and dialled. One ring. She put the receiver down. Waited some more. It took only seconds for it to ring. She let it ring while she wondered what to say.

"Hello," she finally settled on.

"It's me. Are you okay?"

"I'm fine."

"Did you just call me or was that a speed-dial accident?"

"No accident," she said.

Silence. The candle sputtered for a second and threatened to go out.

"Do you want me to come over?" he said.

"Yes."

*****

Abby survives her first day in St. Pete Beach by feigning heat exhaustion. She retreats to the condo to watch daytime TV and lie on the coach with the air conditioning on bust. That night, she waits until the sun starts to go down before she goes out for a swim. The lights in the swimming pool are slowly flickering to life. They glow under the water, turning it a clear, pale green, just like the inside of the marbles Abby used to collect as a child. She swims underwater with her eyes open, swimming toward the light. It is easy to cry unobtrusively in the pool – no one notices red eyes or wet cheeks. Abby starts out diving into the deep end and swimming underwater, where all she can hear is the soft whirr of the pump. Then she switches to lying on her back and using her arms as a headrest. This way the water fills her ears, leaving her with nothing but the steady sound of the air going in and out of her nose.

The pool offers the best view of the sunset. It's a melodramatic, over-the-top kind of sunset. Giant whorls of colour, clouds tinged by intense swirls of deep pink, grey patches stained with orange. The sun is a hot, pink ball. Abby dives underwater for a second, and when she surfaces, it has already disappeared. She dives again and resurfaces with a little splash, startling a man who is walking towards the pool.

"I'm sorry! I didn't see you," he says, clutching his flowered shirt closed. He is wearing swimming trunks and sandals.

"No problem," Abby says, and he smiles then, almost gratefully.

Abby swims to the edge and looks up at him. He is like a lizard, olive-green and shrivelled. The whites of his eyes glow as if he were standing near a black light.

"I'm Abby," she says, sticking her hand up towards him. The lizard crouches down, both legs off to one side, the way Doris does it when she is wearing a skirt and has to stoop down to pick something up. He slides his hand into Abby's. It is cool and dry and smooth.

"Lovely to meet you, Abby. I am Oscar. I live in 223," he says, waving his hand loosely in the direction of his condo.

Abby hauls herself up on the edge of the pool, holding her body up with her arms propped on the tiled surface.

"I'm here visiting my mother, Doris Wheeler," Abby says, but Oscar is already nodding.

"Yes, yes, you're Doris' girl," he says, smiling when Abby grimaces a little. "Oh, yes, darling, you can bet that we've heard all about you!"

Abby shakes her head. Leave it to Doris to issue a bulletin.

"Well, then, I guess you know why I'm here. Recovering from my failed marriage," Abby says.

The lizard offers her a kind smile and pats her wet hand.

"All I know is that you're just a fabulous single gal enjoying a gorgeous week down south!" Oscar says with a wink. "Can I interest you in a cocktail?"

*****

The day that he left was no better or no worse than any other day, Abby tells Oscar over daiquiris by the pool.

She and Michael were lying in bed, arguing in restrained voices about the condition of the highways and whether it was too risky to drive to his parents' house for dinner in this weather. Abby climbed out of bed and peered out into the swirling snow.

"The ploughs haven't even made a cut through Duckworth Street yet," she said over her shoulder to Michael, presenting her case firmly, with only the facts. She knew she stood a better chance of winning if she never let a feeling creep into the argument.

"They will," Michael said and turned over to face the wall.

Abby slipped back into bed and pulled the blanket tight under her chin. She pointed out, in what she believed to be a most neutral tone, that she had wanted to go to his parents' place the week before. But she compromised for his sake and waited. And now look what happened! They probably would not be able to go at all. Michael snorted at her from the other side of the bed.

"Don't talk about compromise! I'm sick to death of compromising. You have no idea how many times I compromise," he hissed.

"That's not a compromise!" she almost shrieked at him. She lowered her voice. "That's a sacrifice! Compromise is when you say what you want and I say what I want and then we do something we can both live with."

She was always better with words than Michael. It annoyed him.

"Yeah, right. We compromise by making sure neither of us gets to do what we want," Michael said.

That was all the fuel that the argument needed. Abby came back with a list of disappointments, and Michael countered with the accusation that she was squeezing the life from him. Soon, he was talking about space and distance and things that involved their being very far apart. Not forever, mind you. "No," he said firmly. He always wanted her to be in his life somehow. But this just wasn't working.

Abby studied the ceiling and chastised herself for splattering some of the sage green paint from the walls onto the pristine white surface. Michael whipped back the blankets and started to put on his clothes. He stood by the door, waiting to see if she would start to cry. She always did, no matter how minor the incident. But Abby decided to deprive him of a chance to be right about her.

"You're not happy, either," he informed her, as if she would have no idea.

"If it makes you feel better to think that, go right ahead. Do whatever works for you," Abby said.

"I'll call you in a couple of weeks. We'll talk then," Michael said, putting a plan in place, making things orderly and neat.

His footsteps on the stairs, a rustle of bags, a tinkle of keys. The door slammed, making it official. Abby expected that she would shatter, explode, and disintegrate into a million tiny shards of misery. But nothing happened. Not even one tear escaped from her closed eyes.

*****

The next night, Oscar invites Abby to join him for dinner at the Don Ce Sar Hotel, a giant, pink palace at the far end of the sand. Doris is excited – the "Don" was all she had ever talked about after her first winter in St. Pete Beach.

"Oh, my Gawd, what are you going to wear?" Doris wants to know.

"A pair of cut-offs and a tank top with no bra?" Abby is feeling almost mischievous today.

"Always the funny one, aren't you!" Doris retorts, but she smiles at Abby's first display of good humour.

After much debate, they agree on a simple sleeveless dress and sandals. Abby indulges her mother by applying lipstick and mascara.

"It's very sweet of Oscar to take you out. And to the Don Ce Sar, no less!" Doris says, fussing with Abby's hair.

"He probably thinks he's going to get lucky," Abby says, with a wicked grin into the mirror.

Doris' hands fly up to her face. She peers out at Abby over the tips of her fingers.

"You don't think? Oh, my, he's older than your father!"

"Not true!" Abby winks in Doris' direction.

Oscar arrives at the condo at eight o'clock and insists on calling a taxi to take them the few blocks to the Don. At the door of the hotel, young men wearing crisp, white shirts and shorts and matching knee socks greet them with charming smiles. They tip their white straw hats at Abby.

At the table, Oscar orders champagne cocktails and offers a toast.

"To shedding your skin," he says, clinking his glass with hers.

"And growing a new one," Abby giggles.

Abby watches as a magician, a darkly handsome Cuban, goes from one table to the next, charming people with disappearing tricks. He appears at their table with a flash of white teeth and asks Abby for her wedding ring. She looks at the band of white gold and tiny diamonds that Michael had chosen for her. It is so simple and beautiful that she can't actually stop wearing it. She shrugs it off her finger, and the magician asks her to place it in a small wooden box. He sweeps a red silk handkerchief over the box with a grand flourish and snaps the fabric out before Abby's eyes. When he opens the box again, it is empty. Abby peers in and sticks the tip of her finger in to touch the velvet lining. She turns to Oscar with a shrug.

"Oh, well, I guess that's a sign if I ever saw one!"

Oscar laughs.

"The signs are never that obvious, my darling!"

Her ring materializes in the magician's open palm. He bows before her and sinks to one knee. Abby laughs, giddy from the champagne and the attention. The magician slides the ring onto the ring finger of her right hand and presses his lips to her fingertips. Abby feels a flicker of electricity from his warm mouth. He looks up at her and smiles. And then he is gone.

"Charming devil," Oscar says with a wink

Oscar is generous with his attention. He wants to know all about her, her life, her work, her passion for painting, her latest adventures in scuba diving. He asks questions, gently prying answers from her when he senses that she is embarrassed by what she has to tell him.

When the jazz trio starts to play during dessert, Oscar asks Abby to dance. She is a little drunk now, the wine from dinner making her body warm and pliant. Oscar takes her hand and guides her to the dance floor. There is something about a man from her father's generation that Abby finds incredibly charming. The quiet self-assurance, nothing showy like young men on the prowl. She likes the feel of his hand on the small of her back as he escorts her to the parquet floor, and the way he anticipates each move as they dance.

Made bold by wine, Abby presses her cheek against Oscar's, rubbing her skin against the crevices in his face. She kisses him, her lips grazing his earlobe. He sighs, a soft rush of air against her ear.

"You're a darling girl," he says.

She pulls away from him to look into his face. He is smiling at her, benignly.

"And you are a lovely man!"

Oscar grips her tightly and swirls her around, as if to execute a dramatic dip. But he pulls her close.

"You're going to get over this, Abby. I promise."

She ducks her head into the crook of his neck.

"You can help me," she says.

"Yes, my sweetheart, I'll be your friend."

"No," Abby says, shaking her head. "That's not what I need."

Oscar hesitates for a second, and this time, he swings Abby around and dips her backward. Her mouth is open in surprise as he draws her back to him.

"Well, darling, it's all a middle-aged queer can offer you," he whispers into her ear as he dances her through the crowd.

The Patron Saint of Hitchhikers

It's Darlene's turn to get them a ride home from the Mall. She scrambles up the side of the embankment, her high heels leaving holes in the tightly packed gravel, and plants herself on the shoulder of the parkway.

"Wait there until I call out to you," she tells Annette and Jackie, and they crouch obediently in the ditch.

Darlene turns to face the traffic with one hip thrust toward the cars and sticks out her thumb, assuming a lazy stance that says, "I've got all night." And they wait.

The traffic is spotty this evening. Dozens of cars sail by in a convoy. Then the road is dark and empty for long stretches. Darlene fishes her cigarettes out of the pocket of her leather bomber jacket and turns her back to the wind to light one. She can hear Annette and Jackie tittering, their soft laughter fluttering up from the ditch. God love them, she thinks, smiling almost benevolently in their direction. They're sweet but gullible. If she told them to wait in the middle of the parkway, with cars zooming past them, close enough to graze their fingertips, they'd probably do that, too.

Somehow, Darlene feels responsible for Jackie and Annette, so she tries to coach them on how to take care of themselves. Often, she can get through to Jackie, giving her advice on how to attract the coolest guys and fend off the roughest girls at school. But Annette is nearly impossible to protect. Her fear is usually telegraphed by her wide eyes, and that makes her fair game for the most vicious girls at school and the older guys on the make.

Darlene can hardly believe that the three of them are the same age. When they turned sixteen last summer, Annette and Jackie went out looking for their first jobs. Annette is now on the Green Crew at McDonald's. She's happy to explain how the crew system works and what you have to do to become a crew leader or Employee of the Month. Jackie works at Zellers, where the cashiers wear name tags and red scarves tied around the necks of their white blouses. The key to standing out is to find a special way to tie your scarf, Jackie says. She favours a floppy bow. They prattle on about what goes on at work, share stories about the cute guys who hang around them and the conversations they had during their breaks. Darlene can't bear to listen to them. She's been working at a convenience store in their neighbourhood ever since she was thirteen. She spends most of her time trying to keep one step ahead of Mr. Hanlon, the guy who owns the place.

"Good thing you're such a looker," he told her when he hired her. "There's no way I'd get away with hiring a youngster unless she looked like she could fake her way into a bar."

Darlene has become a pro at slipping past him in the crowded aisles without brushing against his doughy hands. But there are times when she can't elude his squeezes and his pathetic attempts to rub up against her. It makes her want to puke when she sees him staring at her from across the store, his red-rimmed eyes wide and stunned, his big mouth lolling open. At those moments, she closes her eyes and counts the money that she's been stashing in a pickle jar behind her brother's old hockey gear in the basement. She wants to have enough money to pay for the ferry crossing to Nova Scotia and to get her through until she gets set up in Halifax.

But this job does have its benefits. Working for Mr. Hanlon has helped Darlene develop her negotiating skills. After she'd been there a year, Darlene told him that she had been offered another job. A lie, of course, but it made him sputter and sweat. He upped her wages by fifty cents an hour (more than he paid Dot, the older, full-time cashier) and gave her another shift each week. For three years, Darlene has repeated her threat in a calm, almost bored, voice, and Mr. Hanlon comes through with more money. Jackie and Annette are envious of her riches, convinced that she's got enough money to fly to Los Angeles and buy a whole new wardrobe. Darlene just snorts at them. They have no idea.

*****

Annette is getting tired of crouching in the ditch. She squirms around, trying to get comfortable. But she's wearing new jeans that are way too tight, and she has to keep tugging on the legs to keep them from pinching her crotch. Darlene picked them out for her at Jeans and Things in the Mall and convinced Annette to buy a smaller size. They look cool this way, she insisted. That was a bad idea, Annette concludes. She is also not too sure about hitchhiking this late in the evening. She rarely hitches on her own, only when the bus is late and she needs to get to McDonald's on time for her shift. She did that last Saturday, her thumb held out tentatively as each car whizzed past her on Topsail Road, clouds of exhaust floating back in her face on the cold air.

A brown Dodge Dart passed her and then crawled onto the shoulder of the road up ahead. It's Wayne, she thought, her buddy from work. He is older than Annette, a university guy with dark, wavy hair and cool glasses with tinted lenses. Wayne politely ignores the signs that she's completely infatuated with him. He drives her home from work when they're on the same shift, and every so often, he'll ask her to come along to a movie. They sat at the same table at the Christmas party last week, and Wayne asked her to dance three times. Annette is not sure what this means, but she likes to think it's good.

She jogged to meet Wayne's car, sucking the cold air into her lungs. Her breath was raspy by the time she opened the door, giving Wayne a big smile. The guy inside gave her a wink.

"All out of breath, are ya?" he said, motioning for her to get in.

Annette held the door and stared at him. A skinny, unshaven guy with stringy blond hair, a cigarette held between thumb and index finger. He took a long drag and blew the smoke in her direction.

"Are ya gettin' in or what, my love," he said, giving her the once-over.

She shook her head and stumbled away from the car.

"No. I'm sorry. I thought you were someone else. My friend." The words tumbled out of her mouth.

The guy laughed at her, a high, thin sound that came from his nose.

"Now, my sweetheart, couldn't I be your friend?" he asked, pushing his thin bottom lip into a pout and feigning hurt feelings. "I think we could be real good . . . "

But Annette had already slammed the car door by then and started marching back in the direction she'd come from. That way, he would have had to make a U-turn to catch up with her. Her heart was shuddering in her chest, pounding out a ragged beat. She was afraid to look back until she heard him rev the engine and spin his tires in the gravel before skittering back onto the road. That's when she said a little thank-you to St. Brigid. Her father likes to insist that St. Christopher is the guy who takes care of travel. But her mother is the authority on religious matters, and she always points out that the church cut him from the list of saints back in the 1960s. So that leaves Brigid in charge, a solid, sensible Irish woman who did her share of travelling in dangerous times. The thought of her made Annette's heartbeat slow to a steady rhythm.

*****

"How much longer is this going to take?" Jackie hisses into the darkness.

Her legs are starting to ache. The three of them are wearing shoes, thin, slippery shoes with heels, even though it has been snowing on and off all day. The icy dampness is seeping through to the soles of her feet and up into her legs.

"So, what do you think was going on with Darlene and that guy Alan?" Annette asks, faking a casual tone.

Jackie is peering up towards Darlene, waiting to make the dash.

"Well, they weren't going to his car to listen to the Top Ten at Ten," she snaps back and then immediately feels guilty. Annette is skittish and soft. She must be handled gently.

Earlier in the evening, Alan came up to their table in the food court at the Mall and gave Darlene a little nudge, jerking his head towards the door. She raised her eyebrows at him and flicked her mascara-caked eyelashes up at his face. Then she proceeded to smoke the rest of her cigarette in a slow, deliberate way, keeping him waiting for a little while. Finally, she ground her cigarette into the tiny foil ashtray on the table and stood up.

"I'll be back in a while. Wait for me here," Darlene told them as she walked away with Alan.

Jackie knows that Annette has been running through the possibilities in her head ever since. Was Darlene going to Alan's car to smoke dope? Drink from a flask of Captain Morgan? Have furtive sex in the cramped back seat of Alan's Chevette? Jackie is sure all the options leave Annette equally breathless.

The two of them are simultaneously terrified and dazzled by Darlene. Jackie just does a better job of hiding it. Darlene smokes, drinks and dabbles in every drug that's on the go, like magic mushrooms or a hit of acid. Jackie is embarrassed to admit that she can't really handle her liquor very well. She's become practised at dumping half a bottle of beer or a whole rum and coke down the toilet or into someone else's glass, making everyone believe she's drunk more than she actually has. Annette is not so cool about it. To impress Darlene, she will try to keep up with the rest of the crowd. But she throws up if she goes past three beer or half a bottle of Casel Mendes wine.

But the booze and the drugs aren't the whole reason for Darlene's reputation as a wild girl. The girls at school, especially the rich, snotty ones, like to speculate about the number of guys that Darlene's had sex with. Jackie and Annette have overheard these conversations from behind the closed door of a bathroom stall, heard the glee in a girl's voice as she shared a nasty story about Darlene with her friends. They don't tell Darlene about it because they're afraid of what she'd do.

Darlene likes to hang out with older guys from a hard neighbourhood in the centre of town. They're the types who sell baggies of dope to carloads of people out at the Carpath, a little lane off Thorburn Road. They don't work or go to school. They just hang around the Mall during the day and smoke cigarettes in the food court, daring the security guards to kick them out. A couple of them are good-looking in a dangerous way.

Alan, for example, is the epitome of cool. He has blond hair that curls over the collar of his jacket, his face is all straight edges and sharp angles, and his eyes are blue like the shadow on an iceberg.

"Eyes like Roger Daltrey," says Darlene.

Annette has to ask who Roger Daltrey is, and Darlene gags on the smoke she's just inhaled. She turns to Jackie.

"Does this girl know anything?"

Jackie fills Annette in later on.

"He's the lead singer of the Who."

"Oh right," Annette says, as if she'd simply forgotten.

The guys in Darlene's crowd are all of the same cut – lean bodies, shaggy hair. They wear Levi jeans that have been broken in by regular wear and irregular trips to the washing machine. Jackie is entranced by the way they walk, an easy, rolling gait that says they aren't in a hurry so don't try to make them rush. She admires their lazy grace, their veneer of complete self-confidence. Darlene gives off the same vibe, and it's the power she wields over Jackie and Annette. She is always so damn sure of herself.

*****

Up on the edge of the road, a deep burgundy Impala slows down and glides onto the shoulder. Darlene whistles, two fingers between her lips, and the girls know it's their cue to run up and join her. She is standing beside the open passenger door. The man behind the wheel leans towards the door, his hand spread on the plush upholstery of the seat.

"Get in, girls," he says.

Jackie and Annette get in the back seat, and Darlene slides in next to the driver, lighting up another Du Maurier as soon as she slams the door. The guy's name is Howie, an old guy in a nylon jacket with the crest of his dart league on the sleeve. He has a fringe of hair on either side of the bald spot on the top of his head. The bald spot is shiny and his hair's a little greasy. He's just the sort of guy that Darlene would mock mercilessly. Jackie and Annette giggle into their hands, but they quiet down for a minute to hear what Howie is saying to Darlene.

"So, a pretty girl like you must have a boyfriend. Is he a good fella?" Howie asks.

Darlene flicks back her hair with one hand, soft red hair that's been twirled back from her face with the help of a curling iron. She sucks on her cigarette and lets the smoke snake its way up into her nostrils – a French inhale, it's called. Darlene says older guys think it's sexy. She gives Howie a look, an expression that's meant to convey great sorrow.

"Oh, I wish!" she says. "No, my darling, I don't have a nice boyfriend. I married myself an idiot, a real loser!"

Howie is surprised and looks over at her, trying to re-calculate her age. He must have pegged her for sixteen, eighteen at the oldest. Jackie nudges Annette and rolls her eyes in the direction of the front seat. They know what happens next. Darlene is going to treat Howie to a story about "her husband."

"I took off on him just last week. I was always warning him that I wasn't goin' to take his shit for much longer. I ain't wasting my days washing his filthy drawers and cooking his frigging macaroni and cheese every night," Darlene tells Howie.

"So when he was asleep, I took the money out of his wallet – 50 lousy dollars was all the cheap son of a bitch had – and I packed my bags and cleared outta there. I ain't living in a frigging trailer for the rest of my life," Darlene says, staring out the window at the dark road, fringed with trees.

Jackie shakes her head, astounded by the way the lies drip from Darlene's tongue. It's as if she opens her mouth and says one thing and that little lie breeds and multiplies into a full-fledged pack of lies. Darlene actually lives with her parents and her two brothers in a bungalow down the street from Jackie's place. But Howie doesn't need to know that. He shakes his head.

"No, my darling. You deserves better than that," he says, casting an admiring look at her.

Darlene jabs at the buttons on Howie's radio, changing the stations until she hears a song by Queen.

"Cool," she says and starts singing along to "Crazy Little Thing Called Love."

Darlene bought that record last week at the Mall, and she's come over to Jackie's house almost every afternoon since to play it. She can't play it at home because her father threw her record player through the window and onto the front lawn one night. She says it was because he caught her drinking in the basement. Darlene made Jackie and Annette sing back-up while she pranced around the rec room, snapping her fingers and swinging her hips.

Howie uses his rear-view mirror to peer at the girls in the back seat. He notices that Annette is no longer giggling. She is clinging to the side of the car and squinting out the window at the dark, shiny pavement.

"Aren't you girls a bit nervous about hitching?" he says, throwing the question over his shoulder to Annette. She meets his eyes in the mirror, her mouth wide in alarm.

"I mean they just found that little girl out around Maddox Cove last week. You know, the one who was hitching a ride."

*****

Annette knows all about the girl. She saw her picture on the front page of the *Daily News*. Annette's mother closed her eyes after she read the story and put her curled-up hand to her mouth, wincing as if she were gripped by a sharp and sudden pain in her belly.

"Oh, dear God, that poor little thing," she said. "I'm sure that mother will never get a night of peace again."

She looked up at Annette, who was reading over her shoulder.

"If anything happened to you, they'd have to cart me off to the Waterford," she said.

Annette didn't know what to say to that so she picked up the paper to take a closer look. The girl's junior high school photo was on the front page. She was younger than Annette, only in Grade Nine. She had blonde hair and a round face, a big saucy smile. A family had found her body in the snow when they were out in the woods looking for a Christmas tree. The muddy newsprint had dulled the photo and smeared the edges of the girl's features. But her chin was thrust out in a self-assured way. She did not look like she would scare easily.

Ever since she heard the news, Annette has lain awake at night and imagined the girl lying in a bed of clean, fluffy snow, arms and legs out as if she were making a snow angel. It is so quiet, as if the clearing in the woods is surrounded by a soundproof buffer. Annette can see the girl's blue eyes, open wide and staring up at the navy blue sky, studded with specks of light. Maddox Cove is just far enough away from the city that you can actually see the stars. Annette remembers that from the night Wayne took her for a drive to Cape Spear.

*****

"Nobody messes with me," Darlene is telling Howie. "If some asshole tried to do anything, I'd claw his eyes out."

Annette doesn't doubt that. She can see Darlene's painted nails gouging a red path along a man's face, her tiny hand at his throat, her knee up and into his crotch. It's a brazen quality that Annette longs to have herself. She envies Darlene's certainty about the world.

"I don't hitchhike by myself," Annette pipes up from the back seat.

Howie nods at her in an approving, older-brother way.

"That's good, my darling. You got no idea what kind of losers are out there, waiting to pick up a little girl standing there all on her own and have his way wit' her," Howie says.

Howie is on his way downtown, so he can't take them all the way home. There's light up ahead on the right, a convenience store, and Darlene waves her cigarette towards it.

"Right here is good," she says to Howie.

"Here?" Howie says, looking out at the empty street. "Are you sure about that?"

"Yes, my darling," Darlene says, humouring him. "We travel in a pack. If some guy bugs us, Jackie will distract him, I'll grab him and Annette will rough him up!"

They all laugh at the thought of it. Darlene kisses Howie's cheek as she wriggles across the seat and out the door into the brisk air. Annette and Jackie clamber out behind her.

"Be careful," he calls as Darlene slams the door.

They stand on the sidewalk while Darlene lights up another cigarette. She puffs hard and starts thinking, her forehead creasing with the effort.

"Let's head out to Torbay Road. It shouldn't be hard to get a ride there," she tells the others and heads towards the lights of the main road.

*****

Jackie trails behind with Annette at her side, wondering if they should just feel lucky that Howie was such a sweetheart. Maybe they should walk the rest of the way and forget about flagging down another car. Jackie's father would bar her up in her bedroom if he knew she was climbing into the back seats of strangers' cars. He knows what there is to be afraid of. He's with the Constabulary, been a cop for twenty-three years. At suppertime, he tells them about the cases he's working on, with the identifying details omitted.

"People here are foolish," he says, sawing through his pork chop. "They think nothing bad can happen because this is St. John's."

He stops to put the meat in his mouth and chews for a full minute, as if he must carefully consider his next words.

"If they only knew about half the things that go on in this town."

"What, Daddy? What things?" Jackie's younger sister is twelve and she's eager for the gory details.

"No, my sweetheart, I'd rather you never had to know what I carry around in my head," he says and shakes his head sadly.

In fact, this past week, he was involved in the search for the missing girl. At one point, someone called in with a description of a car that she was seen getting into on Topsail

Road the evening she disappeared. The police collected the licence plate numbers of all the Dodge Darts listed with Motor Vehicle Registration. Then, a bunch of officers divided up the list and started tracking down every one of the cars, knocking on doors and looking for the owners.

Jackie knows this because her father tapped on the door of her bedroom yesterday and asked if he could come in. It was such an unusual request from him that Jackie just stared.

"Sure, Dad," she said finally. "What's up?"

Her father is a big man. He looked awkward in her girly bedroom, sitting precariously on the edge of her twin bed, his knees almost hugging his chest. He told her that the police had tracked one of the cars to a young fellow who lived not too far from their neighbourhood.

"A real pleasant guy," her father said. "Very polite. And he didn't give us any trouble about searching his car."

But the guy got awfully nervous when the police found a little pot of lip gloss under the passenger seat of his car. It was the shiny, gooey stuff that the girls spread on their lips with the tips of their pinkies.

"We asked him where it came from and he said he didn't know. He started pacing around the room and saying he didn't know what it could be. He said he didn't have a girlfriend . . ."

Jackie's father trailed off for a minute. He started again.

"We gave him some time to think, and then, finally, he came up with a name. He said it belonged to your friend Annette."

The guy was Wayne, the heartthrob from McDonald's, the one Annette moons over.

"So what are you saying? You don't think he's the one who killed that girl?" Jackie thought of Wayne's soft, babyish face, his good-boy looks.

"Well, we have no idea who killed that girl," her father admitted sadly. "All we know is that she might have gotten into a car like the one this young Wayne drives. I just think it might be good for Annette to stay clear of him for a while."

Her father was called out the night the girl's body was found. His face fell in on itself after he hung up the phone. He was out all night. Jackie could tell because her mother kept getting out of bed and creeping down to the living room. The next morning, Jackie found him in the kitchen, his head down on the table, cushioned in the crook of his arm. He was sobbing, his body curled into the tabletop, his shoulders quaking. Jackie reached out to touch his arm, opened her mouth to say something. But when he didn't stop crying, she backed away and sneaked out of the kitchen before he knew she was there.

*****

"I think we're close enough to walk," Jackie calls out to Darlene, in what she hopes is a calm voice.

Darlene turns around and stares at Jackie, incredulous. Since when does Jackie offer an opinion about what should happen next?

"I'm freezing my arse off here. I am not walking all the frigging way home tonight," she says and keeps walking.

Annette smiles at Jackie, a weak show of support.

"I'm walking home," Jackie calls out again, louder this time.

By now, Darlene is on the side of the road with her thumb out. Jackie and Annette walk towards her, moving a little faster. They are energized, exhilarated by the idea of defying her. When they catch up with her, she looks at them with narrowed eyes, trying to figure out what their game is. A car slows down, stops and backs up to where they are standing. Darlene walks over and opens the door.

"Are you coming?" she says.

Jackie and Annette look at one another.

"No," Annette says.

"Fuckin' goody-goodies," Darlene spits at them.

The guy in the car is dark and greasy. He leers at her, taking in her tight jeans, the dark eye makeup, the cigarette between her lips.

"Get in, baby," he says. "Looks like it's just you and me."

Darlene gives them one last scornful look and gets into the car. They watch until the tail lights disappear over the top of the hill. Jackie turns to Annette.

"Let's go to the gas station. I'll call my father," she says.

The Song of Bernadette

On the morning of her twentieth wedding anniversary, Helen wakes up early. She squints into the fuzzy, golden light that seeps in through the curtains. Dust motes dance before her, suspended in the air. There is nothing but the sound of Sam snoring, a jagged intake of breath and a shudder as it escapes. He curls towards the wall, his bony knees drawn up towards his belly. The sight of him makes her feel tender. But just for a second. She must get up and get ready.

By three o'clock, most of Sam's extended family and the few surviving members of her clan will crowd into the living room and spill out onto the veranda. They will be joined by Sam's customers, the neighbours, Helen's card club, the nuns from around the corner, and God knows who else. Helen will glide through the house in a somewhat gaudy print dress chosen by her daughter Ellie. She will smile broadly, her thin lips enhanced by Ellie's heavy-handed application of pink lipstick. She will press her homemade sandwiches and cookies on the guests and steer them towards the punch bowl. She will be the placid queen surveying a happy kingdom. But before that happens, there are dozens of chores she must do to make the party a success. Helen shoves her feet into a pair of scuffed moccasins and walks down the hall to find out what all the damn quiet is about.

*****

Helen met Sam because of her friend Doris. They were at Doris' family's summer place in Topsail when Sam arrived to take the flighty and effervescent Doris for a drive. He was dressed smartly in a white shirt and black trousers, and he had his own car, freshly washed and shined. But Doris had gone to the beach with Bernard Whelan just a half-hour before. Helen felt so bad for Sam that she couldn't say no when he asked her if she'd like to go in Doris' place. It was almost the same way when he asked her to marry him. It was not that there was anything wrong with him. Sam was – and is – unfailingly sweet and gentle, a truly fine man. But Helen had never envisioned herself as a bride or a wife or anyone's mother.

All of that happened anyway, each step taking Helen by surprise. She and Sam moved into a little house, with two bedrooms and some space to expand under the sloping roof. Space wasn't an issue the first year they were married. Sam worked all day at his family's store, leaving Helen to paint and practice her music. He rarely stepped inside her studio, knowing it was a place he did not belong. He had little time for paintings.

"Just look out the window if you want to see a flower," he'd tell Helen.

After the first gaggle of children were born, Helen started to feel as if she'd soon suffocate. The house was never meant for a crowd of youngsters. She was always dashing, hands out, trying to catch fragile treasures as they toppled from tables. The children marched through the front room, they climbed on the settee, and they spilled cocoa on the floral carpet, leaving a muddy stain on the pink roses. The house was meant for someone like herself, living on her own.

Helen eventually realized that she'd never be alone again, so she convinced Sam to put in a bid on a bigger house.

*****

Helen shuffles down the hall and pauses at the top of the stairs. It is too quiet. There are six children in this house, and they are usually making a racket. She looks at the clock on the landing below and finds out why. It is not even six o'clock.

In the kitchen, Helen turns on the radio. She makes tea and puts some eggs on to boil for the sandwiches. The news has a report on President Kennedy's reaction to the decision to build a wall between East and West Berlin. She listens carefully to what he has to say. Like many Catholics, Helen sees Kennedy as "our" president. She admires the man's intel-lect and respects his opinion.

In her head, she makes a list of things she can do with the extra time she's won for herself this morning. Bernadette, the second-last child, will wake exactly at 7:15, greeting the day with a series of shrieks. For twelve years, she has served as a painfully shrill alarm clock for the rest of the family. The sound pierces the walls and forces the other children to cower under their pillows. But if Helen gets to the crib just as Bernadette opens her eyes, she can gather the child's brittle, awkward limbs and hold her close, absorbing the cries into her own body.

*****

The morning Bernadette was born, Dr. Howley came into the room and stood by Helen's bed. He began to speak quietly, sombrely.

"Unresponsive," he said. Diminished mental capabilities. Health problems. Special care.

Helen looked at him, getting only a vague sense that this was bad news. She was still exhausted from the sixteen hours of labour.

"The best advice I can give you and Sam is to put the girl in the Children's Home and walk away," he said, as if that were that.

Helen shook her head. She had no idea what was wrong, but she didn't care for Dr. Howley's smug tone. She came home from the hospital and installed Bernadette in the living room, the good room reserved for company. She set up a bassinet on the chesterfield and placed Bernadette there every morning after she was fed and dressed. Sam, meanwhile, remained perplexed. Dr. Howley had cornered him in the hospital lobby and launched into a speech about Bernadette's limited potential. Sam stammered something about consulting Helen and fled. But when he spoke to Helen, he got a cold look and a firm reply.

"What kind of person would put their baby in an institution?" she asked him, and he felt callous and cowardly for even thinking about it.

*****

Billy creeps into the kitchen and grabs Helen from behind, poking his long fingers into her ribs. She swats him with a tea towel, and tries not to encourage him by laughing. Billy is her oldest child and her best. He is her ally, joining her campaign to make Bernadette a regular little girl.

"Hey, Bernie," he'll say, chucking her under the chin. "What are ya saying this morning? Do you have a story for me?"

Billy jollies Bernadette into something that sounds like a chuckle. He'll sit with her and let her hold onto his hand. Her wispy fingers barely make it around his, so he offers her his pinkie. Her nails are long and sharp because Helen can't bear the screeching when she tries to cut them. But Billy doesn't flinch when Bernadette jabs him.

The rest of the children have grown used to Bernadette by now. They call her "the baby" because that's all she's ever been to them. She is no bigger than a two-year-old, but she never manages to do anything that toddlers do. Sean, the youngest, is eight, and sometimes he gets exasperated with Bernadette. He talks to her when he comes home from school and asks her questions. But she just sits there, her head lolling, her tongue out.

"You are so stupid, Bernadette! Mommy, why won't she say something to me?" he'll scream to his mother from the front room, where Bernadette holds court during the day.

"Maybe the cat's got her tongue!" Helen will say, as if Bernadette's silence were just an endearing affectation.

Helen is relentlessly cheerful about Bernadette. She talks to her, filling her head with facts and stories. She laughs and kisses her pale, mottled face and calls her "my beauty." She keeps it up all day long because it's all she can do.

"Give us some of that," Billy says, grabbing one of the sandwiches that Helen has just made.

"They're for the party, you savage," she says, flicking his hands away.

It's just after six o'clock, and Billy is leaving for work. He wants to be an engineer, so he's doing all the courses at Memorial that will get him into Dalhousie in two years. This summer, he's working on a construction project and is already supervising men his father's age. He's meant to be a leader,

Helen says to herself. And then she chastises herself for being too proud.

Billy swings out the door, promising to get off in time for the party. Helen wonders if it's too early for a cigarette. Sam usually leaves her six of them in a bit of tinfoil before he goes to work. During the school year, she gives Billy two of them and a nickel to buy a Pepsi at lunchtime at the university. Helen uses the other four to divide up the day. One before she clears up the breakfast dishes, one after she does the laundry, one after lunch. The last she saves for three o'clock when the girls get home and someone is there to keep an eye out for Bernadette. That's when Helen goes out on the veranda and sits in the shade of the trees.

Since Bernadette was born, that has been Helen's only real contact with the outdoors. She can't leave the house during the day because none of the neighbourhood babysit-ters will stay with Bernadette. Her escape comes at 8 o'clock each evening, after the supper dishes are done and the home-work is under way in the dining room. Bernadette has been put to bed and has wailed herself to sleep. The older children are there just in case. Every night, without fail, Sam walks into the living room with his coat on and Helen's coat draped over his arm. He turns to Helen and says, "I don't suppose the lady would like to go for a drive?" She and Sam sail through the quiet evening streets, sometimes climbing Signal Hill in the darkness to look at the lights flickering over the city. Helen always rolls the window down and lets the wind lick her face.

*****

Helen finishes her last tray of sandwiches and carries them into the pantry with a clean tea towel placed over the top to keep the flies away. Sam has already left for work, placing a dry kiss on her forehead, and assuring her that he'll be home at least an hour before the party is to start. Maureen and Ellie have come downstairs to eat their cereal and beg for a taste of the dessert in the refrigerator. They eventually give up and go to Bannerman Park to sit on the swings and wait for the boys to come around and tease them. At 16, Ellie is the wild one, the child that Helen both admires and fears for her brazen nature. She talks about Del Shannon and Roy Orbison with such a suggestion of intimacy that Helen wondered if they were boys from the neighbourhood. Maureen trails after Ellie in a desperate attempt to have some of her older sister's style rub off on her.

A few minutes later, Aidan races through the kitchen, grabbing a banana from the table as he runs for the door.

"Where's the fire?" Helen calls to him.

"Late for my softball game." His words fly back to Helen over his shoulder.

Helen dashes off a quick list on the back of an envelope, things she needs from the grocery store to finish preparations for this afternoon. When the girls get home, she will send them over to Murphy's on Rawlins Cross to collect the missing items. Helen has done the groceries this way ever since Bernadette was born. She jokes that it's been so long since she entered a grocery store that they probably sell fully prepared meals by now but no one saw fit to tell her!

She starts mixing up the batter for a cake, her hand whipping the eggs into a yellow froth. And then, she looks up at the clock over the kitchen table, and her eyes lock onto its thin, black hands. It is 7:45. She stares down into the mixing bowl and watches the bubbles on the surface pop. Then she goes to the pantry for flour and sugar. By 8 o'clock, the cake is in the oven. By 8:20, Helen has dusted the front room, swept the hallway and put a fresh cloth on the dining room table.

It is almost 8:30 when Helen finally climbs the stairs to the second floor. The carpet in the hallway looks worn, she observes, on her way to Bernadette's room. She puts her hand on the heavy doorknob and turns it. The room is quiet. What did she expect? A chorus of angels? The curtains are still drawn, blocking the sun that usually pours in the windows on this side of the house. She opens them with a quick, jerking motion.

Bernadette lies in her bed, her skin as white and translucent as an empty eggshell held up to the light. For the first time, she actually looks as if she's asleep. Even when her eyes were closed, Bernadette would moan and writhe and wrinkle her forehead as if she was thinking serious thoughts. Helen perches on the edge of the bed and puts a hand on Bernadette's forehead, as if to gauge the progress of a fever. Her skin is cool. She runs a finger along the child's temple, tracing the path of a blue vein.

This is the morning that Helen has been expecting for years. Each time the family celebrates another of Bernadette's birthdays, Helen secretly marvels at her child's longevity. Dr. Howley had warned that "these unfortunate children" don't live long – five, six years at most. But Bernadette has defied him.

Helen pulls the little body to her chest and rocks Bernadette as she has done every morning of her life, singing the hymn that played at her mother's funeral.

"Hail, Queen of Heaven, the Ocean Star," she whispers. "Guide of the wanderer here below!"

For the first time, Bernadette does not resist Helen's comfort. There are no strangled cries, no frantic fingers clawing at her mother's face.

"Thrown on life's surge, we claim thy care. Save us from peril and from woe."

She gently wrestles the child out of her nightgown and into a nice dress, a navy blue sailor dress she was meant to wear at this afternoon's party. Helen sings into Bernadette's ear as she tries to comb the uneven patches of sparse, reddish hair on her head.

"Mother of Christ, Star of the Sea. Pray for the wanderer, pray for me!"

Helen lays Bernadette on her bed and straightens her dress. Then she walks downstairs and picks up the heavy, black receiver of the phone in the hallway. The phone rings in the shop three times before Sam gets to it.

"Molloy's Plumbing and Heating. Good morning!"

"Sam . . . " Helen doesn't want to upset him. He is a sensitive man, takes everything to heart. "Can you get Ernie to watch the shop for you?"

He laughs.

"Don't tell me the guests are there already?"

"No, it's Bernadette. She's gone, Sam."

The bell on the front door of Sam's shop clangs in the background, and someone calls to him.

"Be with you in a second," he calls back to the customer.

"Gone?" he says to Helen, his voice on the line is shaky now.

"Yes, in her sleep."

"I'll be right home."

The party planned for the afternoon turns into an impromptu wake. Father Duggan, Sam's second cousin, arrives first to sit with Sam and Helen in the front room, murmuring prayers and offering counsel. Soon after, two of the nuns slip upstairs and carry Bernadette down from her room. They lay her body out on the chesterfield and cover her bare legs in a hand-knitted baby blanket. One of them drapes a string of rosary beads over her tiny hands. Someone has tracked down the other children, and they flock home to find Helen sitting in the front room. Ellie flings herself into her mother's lap.

"I never even went in to see Bernie this morning," she wails. "I didn't kiss her goodbye!"

Billy presses his mouth into a tight line when he sees Bernadette's still body. He turns to his mother, his shoulders almost scrunching into a shrug. What are we to do now? his eyes are asking Helen. She doesn't know, either.

People stream in to hug and kiss Helen and to grasp Sam's hand in sympathy. But there is an undercurrent of relief in the house. No one will say it aloud, but everyone is grateful for Bernadette's merciful death. The neighbours have long talked of Helen's martyred existence, of Sam's unfailing patience, of the way the other kids pitched in to help with Bernadette.

"What a trial," they would say to one another. "That poor little girl. God love dear Helen."

The funeral passes in a swirl of prayers and hymns. Sam holds Helen's arm as they walk up the aisle at the Basilica, and she can feel him trembling. The children are somber and dignified, most of their crying done in the last two days. The next day, Sam goes back to work – Billy, too, although he must be prodded by Helen and assured that she will be fine.

Helen sits at the table and smokes her cigarette slowly. She stubs it out in the ashtray and walks to the back door. Sean is playing alone in the yard, creating paths in the sand with his trucks. He looks up at her, squinting into the light.

"Are you coming out, Mommy?"

Helen nods and puts one foot on the step, as if testing its sturdiness. Across the yard, the gate that leads to the street stands open.

Touching Down

The combine lies between the highway and a field of wheat. It has been tossed into the ditch like a toy tractor, its metal body twisted and crumpled. Huge bales of wheat are littered over the ground, dropped there as if someone had been called away while moving them. The ground is damp and spongy. It sucks me in as I take each step and coats my sneakers in gritty mud.

The rain began in the middle of the night, sudden and explosive, like a burst of tears. It went on like that for a while, and then subsided, the sky sobbing and shuddering quietly. Just as I drifted back to sleep, it erupted again.

I lay in bed and watched the water sluice down the window pane. David's broad back touched my arm, his skin cool against mine. He's always complaining that I'm too warm. He teases me, touches my skin and pretends to draw back a scorched finger. He calls me his human furnace and jokes about how much money he'd save on heat this winter if I were to stay here.

Sometimes, when our limbs are entangled, he'll pull away.

"You're making me too warm. I'm suffocating in this heat," he'll say.

I get out of bed and open the window a little wider to catch some of the lazy breeze.

The man who farms this stretch of land was moving some of his equipment into the barn during the worst of the storm. The wind ripped part of the roof off the shed and sent jagged pieces of metal and wood flying in wild spirals around the yard. Something struck him in the head and knocked him out. This morning, he's lying in a hospital bed in Regina.

He and his wife are nice people. I met them a couple of weeks ago when I was out this way to shoot some photos for my scrapbook of Canada. A red and white hot-air balloon had just landed in one of their fields. It was an advertising gimmick for a real estate company. The people riding in the balloon jumped out of the bucket and handed Bob and Verna a wicker picnic basket covered in red-checked cloth. Verna pulled back the cloth and peeked in, her face shining like a third-grader anticipating a treat in her lunch box. The basket was filled with all kinds of fancy food – roasted pheasant prepared by the chef at one of the big hotels, three kinds of paté, jars of caviar, a ceramic bowl of fresh strawberries and a bottle of champagne.

"Can you believe it?" Verna asked me, spreading the food out on the round kitchen table, its maple finish scarred from years of family dinners. "I mean, who would ever expect a hot-air balloon to land in their field?"

She poured me a glass of the champagne, and we spread the red caviar onto crackers. I rolled the tiny, salty beads on my tongue. She was giddy, laughing at nothing.

"Imagine us," she said. "Drinking champagne in the middle of the afternoon!"

The newspaper has her photo on the front page this morning. She's staggering into the wind and the rain with her husband's boots on her feet, her eyes wide with terror, her lined face crumpled with pain. I can't look at the photo. I'm embarrassed for her – all that emotion splashed over the page.

I was sleeping, twenty miles away during the worst of the storm. I woke up once to the low moan of thunder.

"Did you hear that?" I whispered, not expecting David to answer.

"It's just thunder," he mumbled into my hair. "It's far away."

I pulled the sheet around me and curled toward him.

"I know," I said. "But it's getting closer."

We had known each other for six days when I moved into his crowded apartment. We were sitting in a coffee shop, eating breakfast. David slid a single key across the table top, through a ring of water left by my glass.

"It's yours," he said, raising one shoulder casually. "If you want it."

I nodded.

"Sure. Why not?"

This stop was not part of my plan. I'd been on the road four months at that point, working my way east to west, taking dozens of rolls of photos. I still had to get to Alberta and then out to the coast. I had friends to visit on Saltspring Island. But, later that day, I hauled my duffel bag and camera gear up three flights of stairs to David's place, a cramped and musty apartment on the top floor of a crumbling old house.

I pushed aside his piles of junk to make room for my stuff. I moved his clothes over to one side in the closet and turned all the hangers in the same direction on the rod. I squeezed his T-shirts and underwear into a couple of drawers in the bureau and pushed my things into the empty spaces. I stacked all of his magazines against the wall of his bedroom. *The Economist. Harper's. Penthouse.*

I'm fascinated by the photos in *Penthouse*. The slim-hipped women with the enormous breasts, sitting ridiculously high on their chests. One day, David comes in while I'm looking at the magazine. I feel like I've been caught, but I don't back down. I hold up one of the centrefolds.

"What do you think of this?" I ask him, pointing at the woman's crotch, her pubic hair shaved into a tiny square. "Do you find this attractive?"

He looks at me warily. He shrugs.

"Sometimes," he says. "Have you seen my baseball glove?"

He plays baseball after supper two evenings a week and then again on Saturday afternoon. Sometimes I sit in the top row of the stands and squint at the field against the fading sunlight. David plays second base. He leans forward, hands on his thighs, watching the pitcher. He looks out of place on the field. He's too big. Barrel chest. Soft, vulnerable beer gut creeping over the waistband of his pants. He should be a football player. I am amazed when I see him lope around the bases, graceful and effortless. It's still hot in the evenings, and he's sticky with sweat when he comes in from the field. We walk home along quiet streets, arms swinging together, fingers linked loosely.

The storm touched down in a small town just miles from the city. The next day, people are out in the street and in their front yards, sweeping up shards of glass and collecting fallen tree branches. Pieces of hail, some the size of walnuts in their shells, still line the gutters, even though the ground is growing warm under the midday sun. I get out of David's pickup truck, grabbing my camera from the seat. A man is turning an elm tree into a pile of firewood, the buzz of his chain saw gnawing at my ears. I ask if I can take some photos.

"I sent Lillian and the babies down into the basement," he tells me. "I was standing by the window and watching it all. And then, out of nowhere, the tree just comes falling in on me. Came right in through the front window."

Just in case I don't believe him, he points at the top half of the tree. It's wedged into an easy chair in front of the living room window, the branches piercing the chair's shiny vinyl.

His next-door neighbours' garage collapsed, crushing their car inside. But they're not fazed by the weather.

"Nothing you can do about a tornado except pray to God," Mr. Williams tells me, his hand gripping a walking cane, its rubberized tip sinking slowly into the soft ground at his feet.

"And it was a tornado," he says firmly. "Don't let that bunch at the weather office tell you anything different. I saw it coming. The sky got all dark, and then I saw the funnel coming across the sky. I knew it was going to take everything that it touched. So we just headed down to the basement and asked God to spare us if it be his will."

He looks at his wife and smiles, his head tilted toward her.

"I guess God wasn't ready for us, was he, Emma?"

"But we're ready – if we have to go," she tells me. "Harold and I have been married for 55 years. We have had more happiness than anyone could rightfully expect out of life."

That evening, David lights the barbeque in the scruffy little yard behind his apartment building. We sit on the step and drink beer. I tell him about the old couple and he smiles, holding the cool bottle to his face.

"Can you imagine being with anyone for 55 years?" he snorts. "What a sentence!"

I get up and poke at the steaks that are spitting and hissing on the grill.

"I thought it was really sweet," I say.

David comes to stand behind me, pulls the hair off my neck and plants a tiny kiss on my damp skin.

"Yes, darlin', but you have no idea of how marriage works," he says, and I can feel his smile, gently mocking me.

The next morning, David wakes me up with a bowl of oatmeal, laced with huge, juicy strawberries, the ones we got at the U-pick just north of the city. He sits on the edge of the bed and drinks his coffee while I eat.

"Your face is getting brown," he says, tracing the pale half-moons under my eyes. "You're looking like a little Indian."

"Very funny," I say.

The night I met David, a drunk in a bar mistook me for an Indian woman. He held my upper arms against the wall in the hallway and pushed his face into mine. His hot, beery breath on my face, the smell of cigarette smoke and sweat clogging my nostrils. He hissed at me, never raising his voice above a whisper.

"Hey, squaw! Your kind aren't allowed in here. Don't you know what we like to do to dirty little Indian whores like you?"

I held my breath, wished I could turn blue. He pressed a line of tiny, oval bruises into my arms. David came walking down the hallway on his way to the bathroom. Big arms curled away from his body. He looked into my face.

"Hey. Hey? What's going on here?" He tapped the guy on the shoulder.

The guy looked up at David.

"Fuck off. I'm just telling the little Indian what I think of her."

David pulled him away from me, and the guy let one of my arms go, then the other.

"Who asked you what you thought?" David said to the guy and pushed him a few feet down the hallway.

The guy lost his footing for a second. He was small and wiry, bouncing on the balls of his feet like a boxer. He looked up at David and decided he couldn't take him. So he staggered away. David turned back to me.

"Don't mind him. He's an idiot," he said.

I nodded, trembling, angry, embarrassed to be so afraid. Why didn't I just push the guy away? Claw his face? Raise my knee into his groin and deliver one swift jab? I didn't want to cry in front of David, the concerned stranger, so I thanked him and pushed the heavy swinging door that led into the women's bathroom. But he was waiting in the hallway when I came out, and he bought me a beer. He taught me how to two-step, whirling me around the rough, wooden dance floor. His solid palm was pressed into my lower back, resting in a curve, steering me this way and that around the other couples. I danced backward and let him lead. Later, he bought me a couple more beer, and I made him laugh when I said he'd be the fella I'd have all my children with.

I finish my oatmeal and drink some of his coffee and throw back the covers.

"Let's go for a ride today," I say.

"I have a game today," he says.

"Skip it. It won't kill you to miss one. Let's just drive somewhere. We'll check into a motel when we get tired."

He looks at me, then at his watch. His game starts in an hour. He's not big on disrupting his routine.

"Okay," he says finally.

We are both quiet as David guides his pickup through the city streets and out onto the highway. Then he snaps on the radio and presses his foot on the accelerator. Burnished wheat waves at us from my side. A field of canola on David's side glows like a buttercup held under a chin. I roll down my window and let my outstretched arm ride on the wind.

"What would you think if I said I wanted to stay?" I call to him over the wind and the music blaring out of the radio.

His eyes never leave the road.

"That would be up to you."

"Yes, I know. But would you be happy if I stayed?"

He says nothing. I count to ten – one, one thousand, two, one thousand, three, one thousand – to give him a chance to answer. He doesn't say anything until two full songs have played on the radio.

"I sure will miss you," he says.

I look out the window. A man is standing in a field near the edge of the highway. He's repairing a fence. He hammers on a piece of grey, splintered wood and nails it back in place. I lean forward and twirl the dial on the radio.

Simple

The phone rings once just after dawn. Donna wakes up slowly, trying to place the sound, make some sense of it. It stops after two rings. She reaches down behind the bedside table and unplugs the phone cord from the wall. The light is starting to creep into the room but Donna ignores it and burrows down under the quilt. She slips back to sleep.

A couple of hours later, Donna sits at the kitchen table, holding one of her mother's china cups in both of her hands and letting the heat seep into her skin. The tea is hot and strong – "barky," her mother would call it and it is laced with evaporated milk that she found in the pantry. Donna savours the syrupy taste, a sweetness she has forgotten after years of living in the city, where people stir fresh milk into their cups.

Everything about the house is the same as it was when she was a child – a fact that Donna finds comforting and surreal. How can nothing ever change here? The house looks like an installation in a museum – Newfoundland outport home, circa 1967. Donna grins at the thought of her mother as the museum interpreter, speaking patiently to the visitors from the mainland about the nuances of making fish and brewis or hooking a rug from old scraps of fabric. There's a souvenir spoon collection on the wall, each spoon hanging from a slot on a wooden cutout of the map of

Newfoundland. The wood stove continues to dominate the room, substantial and solid, its black surface made smooth from years of cooking. Her father's chair is still in its place against a sliver of wall left between two doors. He was always sitting there quietly, his feet hooked around the rungs of the old press-back chair, his eyes taking in the action of the room.

Donna has only been back in the old house for a few days, and she is surprised at how easily she fell into a comfortable rhythm here. Uncle Len, her mother's oldest brother, was the first to show up the day she arrived in town. She was out behind the house, sizing up the shed and wondering if there was any point in trying to salvage it, when she heard his truck out front. Len was trudging around the yard and giving the house a once-over of his own with an eye that's been trained to notice rot in the soffit or a dip in the front steps. She startled him when she rounded the corner, making his head whip around at the sound of her sneakers on the gravel.

"Donna, my sweetheart, how are ya doing?" His face creased up in pleasure and then in sadness."

"I'm okay, Uncle Len," she said, walking into his arms, taking a deep sniff of his jacket – tobacco and cigarette smoke and the faint smell of diesel from his boat.

He stepped back and surveyed her face, looking for evidence that she was feigning bravery.

"Now, are you sure?" he asked.

"Really, I'd rather be busy with the house," she told him firmly.

He smiled then, relieved and proud of the way she is dealing with things.

"You're a grand girl, Donna," he said, giving her another hug that nearly took her off her feet.

All of a sudden he was brisk and ready to get to the business at hand.

"The young fella from up on the point is going to help with the repairs and all," he said, walking towards the house. "Best to start with the outside work. Get at it before the winter comes."

Donna got a notepad and pen from the kitchen, and the two of them spent the rest of the afternoon inspecting clapboard and poking into corners, Len directing and Donna making note of necessary repairs. It gave her a sense of control, a feeling – however false and fleeting – that she was running the show here. But every so often a wave of grief passed over her, a visceral need for her mother's solid, comforting presence.

The man Len had hired showed up just after lunch the next day. Donna was standing at the sink, rinsing her teacup, when she saw him through the window. He was walking up from the main road, keeping a steady pace. There was something familiar about his tall, sturdy body and his gentle, loping gait. He came closer and Donna recognized him as one of the Connolly boys, one of a tribe of six brothers and just as many girls. They had gone to the same school as Donna, but she didn't recognize this guy from the dances at the Legion Hall or the softball field in summertime. He tapped the window in the front door, gently trying to get her attention. When she opened the door, he stepped back to stand a polite distance away.

"Mornin'," he said.

If he had been wearing a hat, Donna was sure he would have tipped it at her. He smiled, nodded in her direction and then looked shyly to his feet.

"Mrs. Andrews?"

"God no! I'm Donna," she laughed and stepped aside to beckon him in.

"Len told me to see Mrs. Andrews," he said uncertainly.

"Yes, I guess that's me," she said and then tried to clarify. "I'm divorced from Mr. Andrews. I think Uncle Len tries to forget that!"

He ducked his head again, embarrassed this time for being slow on the uptake.

"Don't worry about it," Donna said. "Come on in."

He smiled then and came inside, gratefully accepted her offer of a cup of tea. The tea was something new for Donna, who easily consumed a pot of coffee a day at home in Toronto. But she couldn't imagine brewing coffee in her mother's kitchen, any more than she could see herself wearing jeans to her mother's funeral. Besides, there was no coffee machine – let alone an electric grinder for the beans. So the kettle has been filled and re-filled all day as Donna reacquainted her taste buds with the sharp, clean taste of orange pekoe. Donna poured bubbling water into a cup for Tom and nudged the tin of milk toward him.

"I know all of your brothers," she told him, "but I don't believe we've ever met."

"I'm Tom," he told her. "I'm the baby, the afterthought youngster."

Donna remembered her mother mentioning this. Nellie Connolly had had one baby when she was well into her forties, after her other kids were in school. Donna was forty-three herself, and the thought of being pregnant at this point seemed outrageous.

"A brave soul, your mother," Donna chuckled. "How is she?"

"Good, good, she's grand. Still pining for Dad all these years." Tom shook his head, as if he was still perplexed by this. He was silent for a moment and then looked up in alarm.

"Oh, my God, sorry about your mother!" he exclaimed, remembering what had brought him to this house.

"Thanks, Tom." Donna stirred her tea for a moment. "I don't think I ever believed she'd really die. Imagine being so foolish!"

He nodded and stared into his cup of tea, clearly uncomfortable now that he had steered them into emotional territory. Donna got up and brought her cup to the sink. When she turned around, she nearly collided with Tom, who was holding his own cup towards her in both hands, a sweet gesture that made her think of her nephews, Gary's little boys.

"Let's get at it," Donna said, grabbing her list of chores from the top of the fridge.

She led Tom to the yard and gave him a rundown of what needed to be done. He listened to her attentively, his eyes leaving her face only when she pointed at something. With each set of instructions, Tom nodded solemnly and closed his eyes for a moment as if he was recording the details somewhere at the back of his brain. Once Tom started work out back, Donna went inside to get to her own chores. Putting the house in order was the hardest work of all. She did not know how to put her mother's things to rest in boxes and bags. The idea of it made her heavy with sorrow, damp and soggy like the used tea bags piled in the sink.

Donna spent part of the afternoon sorting through her mother's clothes, the print dresses that she wore to church, and the faded cotton shifts that she hauled over her head every morning for housework. They all smelled like her mother, a combination of sweat, Javex and old perfume. One of the drawers in the kitchen was filled with papers and photos, and every piece had a specific emotion attached for Donna. She stacked things in piles on the kitchen table – stuff that she would bring home with her, things to send to her brother and his family in Alberta, and another pile of items that had no obvious place to go.

By the time the day started to dim, Donna decided she'd had enough of the past. She moved to the kitchen and sorted through the groceries she had brought with her until she got some inspiration for supper. Soon, she had the radio tuned to CBC Stereo and was chopping vegetables to the staccato rhythm of a classical march. Curried carrot and apple soup – her mother would choke on the words, let alone the food! Her mother blamed Toronto for all of Donna's acts of non-conformity.

"Curry?" she'd screech. "That's T'ronto for ye. Ye crowd meet up with men with towels on their heads and women snarled up in ten feet of cloth and next thing you know, you're throwing curry into every blessed thing you cook!"

Within half an hour, music was pulsing through the room, and the pot of soup was simmering enthusiastically on the stove. Feeling satisfied with her day's work, Donna poured herself a glass of wine and kicked back in her mother's rocking chair. She had her eyes closed when Tom came tapping on the door. She got to her feet and swung the door open for him, beckoning him in with a broad sweep of her arm. His nose crinkled when he stepped inside and got his first whiff of the curry. But Donna noted that he did not seem displeased by the smell, just curious.

"I'm just making some soup. Would you like to stay and have some?" she asked.

"Thank you, Missus." He creased his brow and then corrected himself. "Thank you Donna! But I got to be getting home. Tonight is fish cakes!"

Fish cakes. They were part of her mother's standard Friday evening supper. Donna's tongue remembered the satisfying blend of potatoes, onion, salt cod and savoury, fried on the pan like chubby hamburger patties until the outsides turned brown.

"Lucky you!" she laughed.

Tom smiled, then turned serious to give her a report on his day's activities, counting off each task on his fingers once he had filled her in on the specifics. He had everything well in hand.

"See you in the mornin'," he called over his shoulder as he walked down the lane, leaving her to her pot of soup and classical music.

Later that night, Donna climbed into her mother's bed feeling a little drunk from the bottle of wine she had consumed over the course of the evening. Her ex-husband, Henry, liked to tease her when she was drunk, using the euphemism favoured by the British tabloids when they spied a politician in an intoxicated state.

"Poor darling, it seems you're tired and emotional this evening!" he would say in a patronizing tone, as if she were a teenager who couldn't handle the lemon gin she had surreptitiously swigged behind the Legion hall.

But now the expression was actually appropriate. Donna curled herself inside a cocoon of heavy handmade quilts and let herself cry for the first time since her mother had died.

The tears seeped into the soft cotton and disappeared, leaving her room to cry some more.

When the sun leaked into the room the next morning, she awoke reluctantly, with puffy eyes and a pounding head. In the kitchen, the shrill whistle of the kettle sliced through her grogginess and shocked her into a temporary state of wakefulness. She stepped out the front door with her teacup in hand, and watched a clutch of birds pecking eagerly at the crimson berries in the dogberry tree in the yard. Leaning on the railing, she studied them with curiosity. Had they always come to feed off this tree?

"That's a purple finch right there on the top branch," came a whisper from just behind her.

Tom walked gingerly across the gravel like a father creeping into a sleeping baby's room.

"And them fellers there?" he pointed. "Them are Bohemian waxwings."

It turned out that Tom could recite more species of birds off the top of his head than Donna had ever known in her whole life. His favourites, it seemed, were the white-throated sparrow, the ivory gull, the red-tail hawk and the lark sparrow. When the birdwatching crowd from the city showed up on the weekends with their binoculars and guidebooks, Tom was always happy to show them around and point out the prime locations for spotting the bird du jour. This week, everyone was waiting for the re-appearance of the yellow-breasted chat.

"How do you know so much?" Donna asked after he gave her a detailed explanation of the migration patterns of several of his special birds.

He stared at her and shook his head.

"I don't know nuttin'," he told her. "Never got my Grade 11."

"So what? You could give lectures at the university about birds!"

"Naw, I'm stunned. Ask me brudders – they'll tell you!"

Donna laughed then.

"Brothers aren't usually very good judges of each other's character. Don't you mind them!" she told him firmly. "You're the bird expert of the Southern Shore as far as I'm concerned."

Tom smiled then and ducked his head, embarrassed by the compliment, but pleased, too, Donna could tell. Once he went to work on repairing the fence, Donna got into her rental car and drove into St. John's to do some errands. She thought about Tom. How charming for a man to deny that he has some special knowledge of an area! Her ex-husband was fond of telling her everything he knew about every subject, from car repair to Thai cooking to economic theory. The truth was: what Henry did best was talk a good line.

On Duckworth Street, she deposited her mother's tax papers at the Revenue Canada office. When she stepped out of the building and turned to look for her car, Donna spied a bird-watcher's speciality shop across the street. The next thing she knew she had spent an outrageous amount of money on a pair of binoculars, a pine birdhouse, a bag of bird-seed and some suet to attract the elusive yellow-breasted chat. She could barely wait to get back to the house and try out her new gear.

In her mother's kitchen, Donna unpacked her purchases on the table, taking the birdhouse out if its box and examining it with the glee of a child at her birthday party. Tom's face appeared in the window of the door while she was leafing through the birding guide, reading the details on the yellow-breasted chat. Without leaving her perch, Donna waved him into the room.

"Listen to this!" Donna commanded, reading from the guide. "The yellow-breasted chat has a very distinctive song. It features a variety of notes that could be described as whistles, clucks and hoots, which form a pattern that sounds like 'cheh-cheh-cheh-cheh'."

Tom stepped into the kitchen, pausing first to wipe his boots on the mat. He leaned in to look at the book in Donna's hands, his expression serious and intent. Donna flipped the pages forward, past the photo of the bird, the brilliant yellow of its breast almost leaping from the page.

"Have you ever heard this song?" she asked Tom. "What about the real high notes – the ones that sound like 'tu-tu-tu-tu'?"

"Just once or twice," he reported solemnly. "It was as good as the girls' singing in the choir down at the church."

Donna laughed at his earnest reply and patted the chair next to her.

"Tell me more."

By the end of the week, Tom had completed the full list of repairs and chores around the house and the property. But he started each day with a birdwatching lesson for Donna, leafing through her guidebook and sharing what he knew about each of the species that were seen along the shore. His instruction was thorough, interspersed with stories of his greatest sightings. But he was willing to listen patiently to Donna's many questions and smile at her interruptions. On Friday morning, Donna greeted Tom with his regular cup of tea (two sugars and just a trickle of milk) and an invitation.

"Would you like to stay for dinner this evening? I'd like to thank you for all your work," she told him.

He shook his head and looked at his boots, obviously confused by the idea.

"No, Missus. No, thank you, Donna," he said.

"I'd really like to thank you," she persisted, gently, though.

"But you're paying me!" he said, as if that made his hesitation clear.

Donna laughed then and changed her approach.

"Look at it this way – you're doing me a favour. I'm dying for some company, and I hate to eat alone," she told him.

She watched as he considered this request.

"That's real nice of you. Okay, thanks." He smiled, showing off the eyetooth that'd been cracked off on an angle.

Later that afternoon, as Tom stacked rotted wood and splintered fence posts in a pile in the backyard, Donna started cooking. The dinner she had in mind was familiar, yet a little adventurous. She had some beautiful cod fillets in the fridge, which she'd bought from a guy up the shore, careful not to question him on the fish's origins. She decided to bake the tender, white flesh beneath a blanket of tomatoes, onions, black olives and garlic and roast the potatoes in olive oil and rosemary. At the last minute, she peeled some carrots and sliced them into coins. Can't go wrong with carrot, she thought.

Dinner was well underway when Tom appeared at the door promptly at six o'clock, knocking as politely as if he were a stranger. He spent a few minutes at the sink, washing up from his day of work. Then he opened a bottle of wine at Donna's urging while she carried the plates from the stove to the table. The first glass of the lovely Merlot she had bought in St. John's sent a tingle through her whole body, and by the time she came to the bottom of the second, Donna was giddy. With his first bite of the fish, Tom closed his eyes and savoured the taste.

"Best cod I ever had," he declared.

Between them, they had finished the second bottle of wine before Donna remembered the dessert, an apple crisp that was warming in the oven. But that was quickly forgotten after Tom tuned the radio to a Newfoundland favourites station and invited Donna to do an old-fashioned waltz around the kitchen. Tom knew how to lead, which made him a rare commodity. He steered her easily around the table, guiding her with subtle pressure from his knee or his palm.

*****

Donna puts her tea cup in the sink and grabs her purse from a chair by the door. She steps out onto the front step and is whipped by a brisk wind. Despite the cold, she walks past the car and heads for the store on foot. Feet crunching on the gravel shoulder, she hurries along the main road, running through a little grocery list in her mind. She will scramble eggs in her mother's cast-iron skillet, brown some leftover potatoes in a bit of oil and onion, and if there's some nice bacon at the store, she will get that, too. She imagines Tom's face as he wanders into the kitchen, following his nose to the table. He will smile as he surveys the table spread with plates of food, a smile that will make her feel warm and content. She left him sleeping under the quilt, curled on his side with one arm thrown over his head. She kissed his shoulder on the spot where the quilt had slipped away and ducked out of the room before he woke.

There are a couple of cars and a pickup truck outside the store. People get up early around here, not because they have to race to work, but because they like the day to unfold in a slow, gradual way. Donna pushes the door open, eager to collect her groceries and get home. Two men are talking to the woman behind the counter. They all turn when she comes in and give her a wave and a nod, just a second's interruption in their intense conversation. She's been here long enough now that she's no longer a novelty, not even worth a long stare anymore. Donna goes to the back of the store in search of bacon.

"Poor old Mary Connolly is nearly off her head with worry," one of the men is saying, his growling voice easily heard over the rumble of the coolers.

"She went into his room this morning and his bed hadn't been slept in," the other man says confidentially.

"The poor old thing." the woman clucks. "Must have given her quite a start!"

They are silent for a moment.

"It's just not like Tom to take off like this. That's what got her so scared. He's always home every night by eleven o'clock," the first guy says.

Donna steps back from the cooler and waits, the package of bacon growing heavy in her hand. She can't look in their direction.

"God love 'im, he's the sweetest fella," the woman says. "He just doesn't have the sense God gave a goose."

The three of them chuckle softly, and they laugh in what they believe is a kind way. The cashier went to school with Donna, though it's hard to tell that they are peers. The woman – her name is Bernie – looks like she's fifty, but an old-looking fifty. She wears a wall of bosom on her chest like an old matron, and her hair is done in a tight perm that leaves her raw, puffy face exposed.

"Maybe I would look like that, too, if I had stayed around here," Donna thinks for moment, feeling an unexpected flash of ferocity towards Bernie. Gotten married young, churned out a few youngsters, got a job in the store or the fish plant, grown prematurely old. Bernie has four children, and the oldest is about to make her a grandmother.

"That would make you look older than your years," Donna tells herself triumphantly.

She makes her way to the front of the store with a carton of eggs and the bacon. The men step back from where they've been leaning and wave her up to the counter, a dramatic, gallant gesture. Bernie extends her chubby hands towards Donna, to take her groceries and ring them in.

"You're up and about early," she says, punching the keys of the cash register, an old one that rumbles after each item.

"Yes, well, lots to do," Donna mumbles.

One of the men speaks up then.

"You know young Tom Connolly," he says. "Hasn't he been doing some work round your mother's place?"

She nods, but does not speak.

"He's gone missing, the poor soul," Bernie says quickly, wanting to be the one to share the news.

"Missing?" Donna repeats dully.

"Yes, he wandered off somewhere," the man says. "He didn't come home last night."

"He's not right in the head," Bernie interjects, to give Donna a sense of the gravity of the situation. "Simple."

Bernie jams the food into a plastic bag and thrusts it into Donna's hands.

"There's a search party getting ready to look for him now," the first man says.

"Then I'm sure they'll find him," Donna replies and turns to leave.

"Be sure to keep your eye out for him," Bernie calls.

"I will," Donna says, but she does not look back.

.

Cathedral Girls

The radio is crackling with calls tonight – drunk and disorderlies, a couple of brawls outside the strip of bars downtown, a few domestic disputes.

"Frigging full moon brings out all the nutcases," Wilf says, and chuckles as if someone is in the patrol car with him.

He has just finished up with a domestic out in the east end. The two cops on the scene called in for backup and, since Wilf was riding solo, he was keen to get in on the action. Dispatch doesn't give you the juicy calls when you're on your own.

The husband had gone psycho on the front lawn when Squires and his partner, a little woman named O'Brien, tried to get him into the patrol car. Wilf heard O'Brien when she called in for help, and she was scared, no doubt about that. Her voice was high and thin as she repeated the call for backup, and Wilf could hear the husband yelling in the background, nearly drowning her out.

"Why have women on the force if they can't hold their own in a domestic?" Wilf asked after he got the call.

He wasn't afraid to ask the question when the women cops were within earshot, even if it meant that they treated him like someone's crazy old grandfather, a man out of step with the times. The story goes that these women cops are good at handling domestics.

"They have the communication skills," the Chief told Wilf, "and they can diffuse tension without having the violence escalate."

"Bullshit," Wilf told him. "There's one way to deal with a guy who's gone cracked and started slapping the missus around. You shove him into the back of the patrol car and take him away till he simmers down."

Wilf figures he does a better job with the battered women than anyone else. He sits beside them on the front step as the other cops drag their husbands away. He puts a comforting arm around their quaking shoulders or pats their knees in a way that tells them they are all right. It's okay now. He's here to protect them. But that approach does not sit well with some of the younger cops. They give him strange looks when he is talking to the battered wives, as if there is something wrong with being nice to them.

These young ones are a different breed of cop. The last ten years or so, they have come to the force with diplomas from the police college. Some of them even have degrees or criminology certificates. They go to university to study the behaviour of the criminal, explore his mind, and try to figure out what he will do next. Wilf doesn't get it. What is there to understand? People will do whatever they can get away with. If they get caught, they will try to blame anyone and everyone for their crimes. Their teenage mothers, their alcoholic fathers, attention deficit disorder, schizophrenia. Every week there is another reason why they're not responsible for their crimes. Wilf sputters each time he hears the legal aid lawyer spinning a new story for a judge. Some of the cops are guilty of it, too. They act as if they are social workers instead of law enforcement officers. Wilf has been on patrol ever since he joined the force, after a couple of years on the traffic beat. He graduated from high school and worked two years at the dockyard before he signed up. He knows what it is to be a cop.

"Marshall? Marshall! Are you awake or what?" The dispatch sounds pissy. It's getting near the end of his shift, too.

He tells Wilf to head up to the Cathedral, where the hookers hang out. There have been a few complaints from the neighbours again about men in cars trolling for a little nasty fun. Wilf guns the car up Church Hill, tapping his fingers on the wheel. The girls who walk the streets in St. John's aren't like the prostitutes in other cities. Not like Toronto – there are whole strips where they work, dolled up in trashy outfits and tottering around in high heels. Not like Regina either, a town that Wilf had visited once for a police conference. The hookers there are tough and desperate, crack addicts and alcoholics who tussle with the competition as often as they do with their pimps. It was nothing to hear about one of them getting killed in a fight over a trick.

Wilf shakes his head. The women in St. John's are sorrowful little creatures who wind up on the streets because they aren't pretty enough to work the hotels, the places where the money is made off the well-to-do johns. It's not just looks either. Some of them are just too old even to be out on the streets. But the ones who really get to Wilf are the girls who aren't all there. They are either a bit simple or screwed up by drugs or booze, or are complete mental cases. They scare him, with their simple-minded fearlessness. They don't have the sense to stay away from the sickos and the freaks, the ones who will smack them around and return them bruised and bloody, or, even worse, the guys who tie them up and burn them with the tip of a cigarette or cut them up with a dull pocket knife.

Wilf's heart races, and he takes the corner a little fast. His headlights swing wildly across the gaggle of girls standing on the sidewalk in front the Cathedral's west door. They look up in alarm and start to scatter until one of them realizes that it's him.

"Hi there, ducky," Lorna calls out to him.

She waddles over, her stretched-out track pants pulled tight over her low-hanging belly. Lorna is always laughing – snorting, sniffling and cackling her way through the night. No matter what anyone says to her – and they can be really mean to the fat girls – she cracks her face open with a bright, eager smile. Many a time, Wilf has found her with a split lip or a bloodied face, crying to break her heart. It's as if she can't believe that the johns, the same guys she is so nice to, could give her a hard time. Wilf tries to warn her, but nothing he says can wipe the smile off her face when she's with him. She is quick to forget what happens when he is not there. Wilf gets out of the car and walks toward the group. Lorna strolls up to him and rubs her big, soft body against his side.

"How's it going tonight, big feller?" she says, running one pudgy, childlike hand along his bicep.

"Not too bad, sweetheart. And what about you? Staying out of trouble?"

Lorna gets a big laugh out of that, and soon the others are gathered around him, giggling, too. They clamour for his attention like schoolgirls with their basketball coach.

"Catch any bad guys tonight?"

Wilf tells them about a fight he broke up down on George Street a few hours ago. That place is a zoo on a Saturday night. The bars run one into the other, turning the whole strip into a street party gone mad. Wilf likes to part the crowd with the front of his cruiser, making the girls giggle as they stumble out of his path. Every night, there is always a guy who likes to show off once he has a dozen beer in him. He is usually the one throwing a few punches over one of those girls, defending her honour or, more likely, ensuring he'll be the one to take her home later that night. Wilf always gets a laugh out of them. There's got to be an easier way to pick up a little dolly, he figures.

The hookers are suitably awed by Wilf's description of the fight and how he stepped between the guys and grabbed them both by the scruff of their necks. They continued to flap their arms in a desperate attempt to get another punch in, but Wilf pushed them away, sending them flying in different directions. Angie waits until he's finished the story before she tugs the arm of his jacket.

"Can it be my turn?" she asks.

She is not even twenty, but when Wilf first saw Angie, he mistook her for twice that. She's already worn out, faded and shredded like an old shirt that's been washed thousands of times. Her blonde hair is burnt and frizzy from too much bleach, and little lines spoke out from the edges of her lips from sucking on cigarettes. She could be really sweet if she just had a nice hairdo and some decent clothes, Wilf thinks. He could see her working behind the counter in a bank or answering the phones in an office.

"Yes, Angie, you're the winner tonight. Let's go for a ride."

She claps her hands like a youngster, delighted to be chosen. She scurries to the passenger door and waits for Wilf to let her in. He always treats them like ladies – holds the door, lights their cigarettes, cleans up his language in their presence. Once she's in the front seat, Angie leans in to the radio and listens carefully to the dispatcher's voice, trying to decipher the calls. She always asks questions about his job, as if she is taking part in a "Bring Your Kid to Work" day. His own daughter never had any time for police work. Natasha calls herself an anarchist, a handle she picked up after she started university, and she tells him that the police are pigs who stomp on people's human rights. They have had many a screaming match about this over the supper table, arguments that ended with Natasha hurling dishes across the kitchen and Wilf retreating silently to the basement to sulk in private.

Angie closes her eyes as she listens.

"What's a M-H-A?"

Wilf smiles patiently. He likes to explain things.

"That's the Mental Health Act. Say if a fella is gone mad and we think he's gonna hurt hisself or somebody else, then we can take him in."

Angie raises her pencil-thin eyebrows and laughs.

"Really? I wish somebody woulda told the cops about my old man! He was always going off his head and beating the shit out of us!"

Wilf imagines his fist connecting with the bastard's face.

"Let's go down by Quidi Vidi Lake tonight," he tells Angie. "For a little change."

A few years back, Wilf took the first of the Cathedral girls out for a late-night ride. He guided his patrol car up the curving road to Signal Hill because he wanted to show Nellie how beautiful the city looked at night, the lights below them sparkling in the velvety darkness. When he was a young buck, Signal Hill was the prime location to go parking with a girl. But that night, he felt like a tourist guide as he sailed up the hill with poor old Nellie in the car beside him. She was a sad, wrung-out woman who had lost two kids to Child Welfare. When they reached the top, Wilf pointed to the lighthouse winking from Cape Spear. He told her stories about Marconi and the first wireless message that he received at Cabot Tower. She smiled politely, her thin lips barely turning up at the corners. Wilf was confused when she slid across the seat and tugged expertly at his belt buckle. He protested and pushed her head away.

"Hey, now," he said, trying to sound authoritative. But he went silent after she unzipped the dark blue pants of his police uniform.

Wilf drives to the head of the lake, a section where traffic is minimal at this time of night. Angie jabbers away beside him, filling him in on the intrigue at her rooming house. Always some kind of drama going on there – someone stabbing someone else over a half case of beer, Wilf recalls. He's answered calls at that place a couple of times this summer. The first time, Angie came running out of the house and into his arms, wailing like a baby. The other cop on the scene had to wait until Wilf could pry Angie's arms from around his neck before they could go into the house. The place was a dump. Ratty chairs with the fabric torn away from the arms. A table with wobbly legs leaning towards the wall. Cases of empties stacked in the hallway, waiting to be exchanged for a half-dozen beer at the corner store. And the smell of piss and vomit in the hallway. It made Wilf want to puke himself once he realized that this was how that poor little girl lived.

Angie's wet mouth on his penis snaps him back to his cruiser parked by the lake. He looks down, momentarily confused as he watches her blonde head bob over his lap. She had moved across the seat without a word. He leans back against the plush fabric of the headrest and closes his eyes.

On the way back from the lake, Wilf stops at Tim Horton's. He orders a large coffee laced with cream and watches as Angie casts a greedy eye over the trays of donuts. They are glossy with chocolate and sugary glazes, dancing and shimmering under the lights. As always, she will survey every item before she settles on something.

"Can I have one of the fancy ones out front?" Angie asks, her face pressed close to the glass.

"Whatever you want, my darling," Wilf says. "It's your night."

She smiles up at him from her spot in front of the display case. He is embarrassed to have pleased her with so little effort. They sit side by side at the counter to drink their coffees. Angie jams the bowtie donut into her mouth as if someone may grab it from her.

On the way out of the parking lot, Wilf passes another cruiser on its way in. Squires and O'Brien on their way back from the domestic. O'Brien stares at him; her head swivels to follow his car as it slides out onto the street.

*****

When Wilf walks into the station at the end of his shift a few days later, the clerk at the front desk has a message for him.

"The Chief would like to see you. Now," the clerk says, sorting through a pile of papers on his desk and handing Wilf a pink message slip.

The Chief's secretary is a pretty girl, very friendly. She and Wilf always have a good laugh any time he passes through the main office. This afternoon, she greets him with a distracted look and stabs at the intercom button on her phone to let the Chief know he is here. Wilf strides toward the Chief's office, carefully tucking his shirt into his pants as he walks.

"Hello there, Chief! Good to see ya," Wilf says, with the familiarity of a man who's been around for a while.

The Chief nods.

"Afternoon, Constable Marshall."

He jerks his head at the man sitting across the room.

"You know Constable Green from the union."

Wilf winks at Green.

"How's it going, brother?"

Wilf likes to talk the union lingo with the boys. But Green just nods and doesn't even crack a smile. He looks pained, shifting in his chair like a boy waiting in the principal's office. The Chief leans forward in his chair and picks up a piece of paper, reading it over the top of his glasses. Finally, he looks up at Wilf.

"We got a bit of a problem here."

The meeting takes only a half hour. When Wilf leaves the station, he is wearing his regular clothes, a pair of khakis and a golf shirt. His uniform is hanging in his locker. Out in the parking lot, he stands by his car and lights a cigarette. The view from here is great, he notices. The evening sky over the Southside Hills is rosy and warm. Wilf looks at his watch and wonders if there's any point in going home right now. No, he decides. There's no point at all. Instead, he gets in his car and drives east on his way to the Cathedral.

Going Home

The tumour was bigger than the little oranges that Margaret ordered from the church every Christmas. She watched Dr. Furey's eyes as the nurse helped her ease the cotton hospital gown off her shoulder. He tried to maintain a neutral expression as he pressed his fingertips in rapid circles over her left breast.

"You've had this lump for quite some time."

Margaret wondered if she should lie, pretend she'd never even noticed it. He would probably think she was cracked, gone in the head like some of the other women who lived in the home with her. They couldn't remember what was trumps when they were playing cards. One of them was prone to leaping from the supper table and accusing everyone else of robbing the turkey from her plate. Margaret bubbled with rage each time it happened to another one of them, when they started losing their minds. She complained to her daughter, but Ella was no help. Ella, the nurse, had an explanation for this wacky behaviour that absolved them of blame. But Margaret just wanted them to pull themselves together and get on with it.

"Yes, for a while," she admitted to Dr. Furey, he of the charming blue eyes and winning ways. "But I didn't realize that it was getting bigger."

"Mmmm, I see," he said, examining her deformed breast from various angles.

"I don't s'pose it could be cancer," Margaret said, as if she had just thought of the idea.

Having said the word aloud was almost a comfort to her. She had been spinning the idea of cancer in her mind, and it expanded as it whirled, turning into something huge and growing and completely unmanageable. Cancer made her think of rot, organs corroding, skin eating itself from the inside out, her body falling to pieces in front of her eyes.

Dr. Furey raised his eyebrows, silently asking if she was kidding.

"Mrs. Kelly, I've seen a lot of breast cancer, and I am pretty sure that's what we're dealing with here," he told her in a calm voice.

Dr. Furey loves women – it's clear in the way he looks at them, talks to them. It was part of the reason he became a specialist in breast cancer. He admires their courage and is touched by their vanity, their fear of losing their beauty once their bodies have been damaged by cancer. He sat down on the stool in front of Margaret and took her hand between both of his.

"Mrs. Kelly, you're a beautiful woman, so full of life," he said.

Margaret could not help herself from basking in Dr. Furey's charm. She smiled at him for a moment and indulged his interest in keeping her healthy.

"That's why I think we need to take this tumour now and let you get back to your life," he said, rubbing her hand.

She nodded politely. But she wasn't listening. Margaret had been waiting for news like this, a clear diagnosis that would speed her death, something she had been praying for, ever since she lost Joe. She had long insisted that she would have no surgeries, nothing extraordinary to extend her life if she became sick. It was a relief to have already formulated her response to this new situation.

*****

Dan Healey had come home from New York City the summer that Margaret was 13. She heard her grandparents discussing it at the kitchen table, Grannie's voice a shrill whisper and Pop's a low growl. Margaret was flung across the daybed with a book hovering over her face.

"Don't you go telling Sadie that he's here," Grannie hissed.

"Good Jesus in heaven! Everyone in Salmonier will soon know he's here," Pop sputtered. "You'll not be able to keep it from her for very long."

Sadie, Margaret's mother, lived out the road with her husband, Mr. Jack, and their three children. She had her hand in everything that went on in town, from running the local store to birthing babies to organizing the church garden party that was scheduled for that afternoon. Margaret had always lived with her grandparents. This never bothered her, despite the taunts from her saucy cousin, Eddie. Truth be told, Margaret was just as happy where she was. She was an only child of sorts, never forced to share her grandparents' attention. And they gave Margaret everything she wanted, although they never let on that it was happening.

"Pop, when are we going over to the garden party?" Margaret whined from behind her book.

"Soon, my sweetheart, soon," Pop said and glared across the table at Grannie.

Grannie supervised Margaret as she got ready to go. She coaxed Margaret's fine brown hair away from her face with a narrow hairband of blue satin. Standing at the wardrobe in her bedroom, Grannie extracted a blue cotton dress from the spot where it was wedged among the other clothes. She held it up before her and used her hand to iron out the wrinkles.

"What do you think? Will it do for a princess like yourself?" Grannie asked Margaret in a teasing voice that tried for gruffness.

When they got to the garden party, Margaret's eyes raced through the crowd, looking for her friends, her mother, anyone who could take in her beautiful new dress. She saw Sadie directing some of the other church ladies, her hands flying in the air as she showed them where to lay bowls of potato salad and plates of turkey and ham.

A man walked up to Sadie and nodded at her politely, his hands clasped behind his back. He wore a white shirt, clean and neatly pressed, and dark pants. City clothes, Margaret thought, although she had barely been to a city. Sadie looked up at him, and her face almost instantly reddened, two bright spots high on her cheeks. They talked, lips moving in a flurry, eyes never leaving the other's face. Margaret had never seen him before, but she was instantly fascinated. No one could ever rattle Sadie.

Margaret picked her way through the crowd, dodging old ladies and toddlers as she headed for Sadie and the stranger. Just as she got near them, Sadie looked up and caught a glimpse of Margaret. She said something to the man, and his eyes darted towards Margaret. Margaret was delighted that her new dress seemed to be generating so much attention.

Sadie extended her arm towards Margaret, beckoning her to come close. She put one hand on Margaret's shoulder, a hand that was always firm and steady, but now was trembling.

"Mr. Dan Healey, I'd like to present to you my eldest daughter, Margaret Ann," Sadie said, sounding as proper as someone doing a reading from the Bible.

He smiled and Margaret was immediately charmed. His eyes danced, and his grin was saucy and a bit devilish.

"Well, Margaret, aren't you a fine young lady!" he exclaimed, causing her to blush as red as Sadie.

"Pleased to meet you, sir," she said, ducking her head to hide her flaming cheeks.

"No, it is definitely my pleasure! I've been waiting for some time to meet you," he said, solemn now.

Margaret looked up at Sadie, confused, but her mother only nodded. Dan Healey bent down a little so that his face was level with Margaret's. He placed one hand on her shoulder.

"Your mother and I are very old friends, Margaret. But I moved away to live in New York many years ago," he told her.

New York City? Margaret had heard stories about this mythic place.

"You're welcome to come and visit me some time if you would like," he smiled at her.

"Oh, I would like to! Very much!" Margaret turned to her mother. "Can I?"

"Oh, Dan, don't say that!" Sadie burst out. "You know they won't stand for that. They would never let her go!"

Dan's face changed for an instant from charming to cold.

"Sadie, it's not for them to say. She is not their child," he said, biting off each word.

But Sadie cut him off before he could continue.

"I think it's time for us to sit down and eat," Sadie said, moving them both toward the supper tables. "Let's all go and enjoy the garden party. We'll talk about this later."

Dan smiled at Margaret and offered her a wink that told her they were in this together. During the meal, Dan sat across from Margaret, chatting amiably with everyone around him. She watched him carefully, looking for any further exchanges between him and Sadie. After the food was cleared away, the Hawco brothers got up with the fiddle and accordion and started the music. Couples found each other and slipped through the crowd to the makeshift dance floor. One of cousin Eddie's friends asked Margaret to dance, and they stumbled around the floor, laughing as they trod on one another's toes.

Over the boy's shoulder, Margaret watched as Dan Healey approached Sadie with his hand extended. They walked onto the dance floor, her arm hooked through his. Grannie saw them first and looked wildly around the yard for Pop. A number of heads swivelled in Dan and Sadie's direction, and soon people were jabbing their elbows into the ribs of the people next to them. The crowd watched as they waltzed through the other dancers with the ease of a couple marking their 50th wedding anniversary. Grannie and Pop stood off to one side, taking in the drama with grim faces. Mr. Jack, Sadie's husband, hung back from the rest of the crowd. His head was averted at the moment when Dan Healey leaned in and kissed Sadie full on the lips.

Margaret stayed out for one more dance, craning her neck to see what Sadie and Dan Healey were up to next. By the time she came in from the dance floor, Grannie informed her that it was time to go. She was raging, Margaret could tell. Grannie did not say one word on the way home from the garden party. Pop kept up a running commentary on every aspect of the event, from the food to the music to the clothing sported by some of the women. He kept Margaret giggling by imitating a few of the most colourful characters in the parish. Back at home, Grannie took off her hat and put it away before she stomped up the stairs to her room.

"I think we'd best lie low till she cools off," Pop said to Margaret with a wink.

"What's got her so mad?" Margaret wanted to know, even though she knew for a fact that Dan Healey was involved.

But Pop shook his head and went outside for a smoke on the back step. In her own room, Margaret got into her night-gown and hung her new dress on a hook on the back of her door. She climbed into bed to read and was almost asleep when she heard Pop and Grannie arguing in their room.

"I will not stay quiet, and don't you tell me so," Grannie hissed.

"Why can't you just let it go? You got what you wanted for Sadie. What difference does it make now?"

"It makes all kinds of difference. I don't want that little girl traipsing off to New York and getting ideas about leaving us and going to live there with him!"

"She's not a little girl, Maisie. And she's not always going to want to stay put with you."

"Maybe not, but I won't have her going to live with him!"

"For the love of Christ, he's not an axe murderer. He's the girl's father!"

"Now you be quiet, Stan! Just shut your mouth!"

It took a few minutes for Margaret to consider what she had just heard. Of course, it made perfect sense. Everything clicked into place for her – her mother's new family, the jokes that the other kids made about her living with Grannie and Pop. Margaret had never thought she was missing out on any-thing by living with her grandparents. But the minute she knew of her father's existence, she felt his absence.

*****

The x-ray technician at the Grace Hospital welcomed Margaret as if she were holding a party at her house and Margaret was the special guest.

"Hello, my love! Come on in," she said, holding the heavy swinging door open with her hip.

Margaret offered her a smile as thin as skim milk. She had been at the hospital since ten this morning, and all she wanted was to sit down and relax for a minute. No more of this climbing up on examining tables and getting undressed for strangers.

"Now, my darling, you can go in this little room here and get changed," the technician said, directing Margaret towards a cubicle and handing her a hospital gown.

Margaret held the gown in her hand and rubbed the thin cotton between her fingers. Not much to cover a body with. She couldn't bear the thought of shrugging off her coat again and wrestling herself out of her blouse. She sighed, a soft shuddering sound. The technician, a young blonde girl, looked alarmed.

"Are you all right, my darling?" she asked, smoothing Margaret's shoulder with a warm hand.

Margaret shook her head, but she couldn't think of what to say. The door flew open, propelled by a push from Margaret's granddaughter, Connie.

"Sorry, Nan," she said in a rush of breath. "Couldn't get a parking spot!"

It's okay now, Margaret decided. Connie would chatter with the technician, ask a million questions, ease Margaret out of her coat and her blouse and then into the dreaded hospital gown. Margaret would simply need to make her body pliant and her mind empty. She shut her eyes and listened to the chatter – just the sound, not the actual words. She opened them for a moment to watch as Connie talked to the technician, her hands flying with every phrase. Margaret marvelled at Connie. All that talking. It must be a gift! Then, Connie was steering her firmly towards the cubicle, with the cotton gown slung over her arm. She closed the door, hung up Margaret's coat on the metal hook, and efficiently unbuttoned the blouse.

"It'll be no trouble, Nan. Just get a few snaps taken in front of the x-ray machine and then we'll be outta here."

Margaret winced as Connie tugged gently on her arm to get it into the sleeve of the hospital gown. Her right shoulder was crippled by bursitis, an insulting reminder of her ninety years. It made it harder and harder to get dressed on her own. But Connie sorted it out. Finally, Margaret shuffled to the room that housed the large, upright x-ray machine. The technician hefted the x-ray plates from the shelves to the machine, her young, sturdy back unfazed by their weight.

"Now, my darling, just come right here and lift up your arms for me," the girl said, beckoning Margaret toward the machine. But once she stood in place, Margaret could barely raise her right arm, let alone hold it there.

"Here, ducky, come over and help your nan," the technician said, waving Connie to a spot in front of Margaret.

The technician helped Connie put on a heavy, protective vest and showed her where to stand. She faced her grandmother and picked up each of her soft, wrinkled hands. Connie lifted them gently and rested them on her own shoulders. They stood staring right into each other's faces. Connie smiled and gave her grandmother a saucy wink.

"Yes, that's right, that's just perfect," the technician exclaimed, like an enthusiastic photographer.

She pushed a button and the old x-ray machine rumbled as it captured the image.

"See?" Connie said. "We're done!"

*****

Margaret climbed down off the wharf, her good summer coat pulled around her legs. Her cousin Eddie stood in the dory below and put out a hand to help her down. It was not easy. She was wearing a dress that she and Grannie had made especially for the first day of her new job. A good, smooth cotton, printed with tiny flowers. Her shoes were new, too, and slippery on the soles. They were not meant for clambering around wharves and boats, slick painted surfaces, greasy with rain.

Eddie had agreed, with some prodding from Grannie, to take her to North Harbour in time for the first day of school. He was a year older than her, but he had left school at 14 to fish with his father. So he had little time for Margaret and her fancy teaching job and her fine education.

This job was a complete surprise to Margaret. She had gone to confession the Saturday before, as always. There were three people ahead of her – her cousin Annie, Mrs. Collier, from out the road, and old Mr. Bennett. Margaret gave them three minutes each (a little extra for Mrs. Collier because she liked to talk up her sins a bit) and figured she had about ten minutes to compose her own list. She supposed thinking up sins was sinful in and of itself. But, some days, she was hard-pressed to believe she had done anything terribly bad.

Just to confirm this, Margaret counted off her good deeds on her left hand: baking the bread for her grandmother, doing the wash and heavy cleaning, bringing in the wood from out back, and reading from the Bible to her grandparents every night before bed. The worst that could be said of her was that she was a bit vain, a little too concerned about her hair, her dresses, and the way she looked.

With that, Margaret forgot about her sinning and wondered what she could do to improve last year's dress for the dance that night. There was a handful of fake pearl buttons she had found in a jar in Grannie's pantry. She could sew them in a smart line down the front of the bodice. That would make it look altogether different. And no one would remember when she had worn it last.

She looked up with a start as she heard Mr. Bennett banging in frustration at the door of the confessional. As usual, he was pushing the side with the hinges on it and bleating about how it was stuck. Margaret got up and pulled it open for him from the right side. He stepped out and blinked in the dimness, surprised to see her. Then he turned and shuffled down the aisle toward the altar.

Margaret stepped into the confession box and knelt down to wait for Father Molloy. She could hear his raspy, congested breathing even before he pushed across the wooden, latticed window between them. Margaret looked at his face in profile, noticing how very big his nose had grown. "It's from all the drink," Grannie hissed at her once when she asked why. But Margaret was not supposed to let on that she knew that.

Margaret and Father Molloy went through the routine. She offered up a speedy rendition of the Confiteor and claimed to have been impertinent to her Grannie. Father Molloy mumbled and waved his hand in front of her, and sentenced her to ten Hail Marys on her knees up at the altar. But when she stood up to leave, Father Molloy cleared his throat. She waited for a moment and then put her knees back down on the smooth wood.

"Margaret, there's a teaching position in North Harbour this year. Mrs. Hall has retired. If you go over on Sunday, you'll have just enough time to open up the schoolhouse and air it out and get ready for classes," he said.

She said nothing, even though she knew that was not the right response.

"I have talked to a very nice family there, the Boones. They have no children of their own, so they told me they would be pleased to have you board with them," he continued.

Margaret studied her hands and wondered what would make that rough, red skin turn smooth and pink again.

"Do you have any questions, Miss Power?" Father Molloy said after the silence went on too long for his liking.

She shook her head and started to stand up.

"Don't you have something to say, Miss Power?" he said, and she realized she had gone too far with her silence. He would be by to see Grannie before the night was out if she didn't smarten up.

"Yes, Father. Thank you very much, Father," she said primly and, she hoped, piously.

"It's just . . . I was a little surprised," she offered lamely.

He snorted from behind the lattice.

"I can't imagine why. You had the highest leaving marks of anyone in the district," he said and pulled the window shut with a thud.

And Margaret knew that was that. So there she was, sitting in a dory with Eddie on the way to her first job. A light drizzle hung over them, clinging to the outlines of their bodies. Margaret sat with her knees pressed together, holding the edges of her coat away from the water that was slopping around the bottom of the dory. She felt an icy dampness in her feet and looked down at the murky water that was creeping up around the tops of her new shoes. Grannie gave Margaret a hard time about them and complained for a half hour about how much they cost and how easily the smooth leather would get scuffed and marked as soon as she stepped into the classroom.

"Eddie, we're taking on more water," she told her cousin.

"Nawwwww," he said and kept on rowing, his face red from the effort and the cold.

Soon, the water edged up around his ankles, but he didn't notice because he was wearing his rubbers. Margaret put her feet up on the seat in front of her. Eddie looked down at the water swirling around his feet.

"Jesus, Margaret, we're taking on water," he bawled at her.

"For the love of God! I told you that," she bawled back.

"Well, you'd better find something to plug that hole or we're going down," he yelled out of the side of his mouth.

Margaret looked around the bottom of the boat. There was nothing. So she shrugged off her new coat and ripped out the lining with a quick jerking motion. She balled up the silky fabric and crammed it into the space where the water was coming in.

"There," she screeched at Eddie.

He looked at the hole and then back at her.

"Well, now. Not too bad, Miss Margaret," he said.

*****

Ella put on the kettle for a cup of tea and set out a plate of tea buns (from the supermarket bakery, Margaret noted). Margaret told her about the woman who had died on Sunday and was now waking in Dunphy's funeral home, decked out in the dress her children had bought her for Christmas. Margaret sent her words in a steady stream towards the back of Ella's head as she stood at the counter, waiting for the water to boil.

"So Patrick says to Bride, 'I'm going out into the yard to gather a few strawberries for you off that bush.' And he takes off his slippers and he puts on his shoes. And he tells her, 'I won't be more than five minutes.' And she says, 'I don't care how long it takes. Just be ready in time to drive me to bingo'."

Margaret paused then, a quiet moment that was full of drama and anticipation. Ella was stiff, her shoulders raised, leaving her looking as if she had no neck.

"And didn't he come back not ten minutes later and there she was laid out on the kitchen floor, with her coat on and her purse in her hand. Patrick took one look at her and he knew that was the end of her."

Margaret stopped and folded her hands in front of her on the kitchen table. She waited for Ella's response.

"Go on?" Ella said finally, without much enthusiasm. "As quick as that."

"As quick as that!" Margaret confirmed.

She gave Ella the details on Bride's dress, the one she was wearing in her coffin. It was a dark green jersey knit with a handful of gold buttons marching down the front. Not that the dress unbuttoned. It was just for the effect. Ella sighed, a sound like air rushing out of a punctured tire. She knew where this conversation was headed. It used to be a minor annoyance, an amusing routine of her mother's. But since the diagnosis, Margaret's talk of dying made Ella scared.

"Now, Ella, when it's my time to go home, to be with Daddy, I want to wear my good dress," she said.

The good dress was not a specific dress. It changed depending on what Margaret got for her birthday or Mother's Day or Christmas.

"You know the one I mean?" Margaret said.

"No, Mom. Which dress is it now?" Ella said, but she did not turn around.

Margaret's face shrivelled. She stared at Ella's back and said nothing for a moment.

"I told you," she said, a little whiney now. "The blue one that Connie gave me for my birthday."

"Forget about the dress! You are *not* going to die." Ella's voice was fierce.

Ella watched her mother's reflection in the window, the surprised look on her face.

*****

Every day after lunch, Margaret moved slowly down the hallway to her room to say her prayers. A decade of the rosary, low murmurs to herself. Then she lay down awhile to be with her man. She is with Joe much of the time she's asleep. Nothing fancy or dramatic. Sometimes they're just eating supper at the kitchen table, well after the last child has left the house. Or they're getting out of bed at midnight and walking out the road to the Star of the Sea to catch the last set of reels at the dance. Or further back, she and Joe sitting on the back steps, watching the children run and fight and tumble in the yard. The thought of him makes her feel warm, as if his arm were still thrown around her as she slept, as if his short, solid body were still curled against her back.

Joe had not been the first man in her life. But he was the one who stuck. She had her pick of the young fellows in North Harbour when she was teaching there. They made their way to Mr. Boone's house as soon as she moved in, and one of them was always perched on a chair in the kitchen or waiting for her on the front step.

"Margaret Ann Power, you have a gentleman caller," Mr. Boone would sing out to her from the kitchen, his voice carrying far enough for the neighbours to hear.

He would torment her with embarrassing stories while the young men were visiting, saying anything that he thought would bring the colour to her cheeks. Each caller had to endure at least a half hour of Mr. Boone's teasing before he could leave the house with Margaret on his arm. They rowed her across the harbour in a dory to the dances. Or they would take her for dinner at their families' homes on Sunday. Who wouldn't want the stylish young schoolteacher gracing their dinner table?

But the schools became casualties of the Depression after Margaret's second year of teaching, and she was out looking for work. She ended up doing housework at Nancy Hawco's little hotel, a job that frustrated her most days. It was not that she thought she was too good for cleaning and cooking. Margaret just wanted to do it her way – running the kitchen efficiently and making the rooms comfortable and presentable. The day she met Joe, she was actively plotting her escape. He arrived at the back door of the hotel and knocked. When she opened it, she saw exactly what she wanted for the rest of her life. A sturdy man, not much taller than herself, sporting a head of gorgeous wavy hair. She touched her own hair, fine and wispy, and thought it was ridiculously unfair for a man to have such abundance.

"Margaret Power?"

"That would be me."

"I'm Joe Kelly. I hear you might be looking for a new job. And I need someone."

That was it. Margaret was gleeful when she told Mrs. Hawco to find herself a new slave to do her bidding. She went to work at Joe's house, taking care of his four younger siblings, children who had been left in his care when his parents died one after the other in the two years before. The children greeted her with a mix of relief and suspicion. The eldest, a frail, gentle fellow named Anthony, migrated to her side and became her silent companion. On the day she arrived at the house, Anthony had taken it upon himself to bake a cake in her honour, which he presented after their first dinner together. The littlest girl was only six, and she scrambled into Margaret's lap as soon as she took a seat. But the older girl, Lizzie, was old enough to have clear memories of her mother and to resent her early passing. She looked at Margaret through hooded eyes, wondering what she was doing baking bread in her mother's oven.

Margaret's shift from housekeeper to wife was so subtle that it barely registered on Margaret and Joe themselves, let alone the rest of the family or the people in town. One evening Joe laid his hand on her shoulder as she did the rest of the supper dishes and asked if she would come and sit with him on the veranda. After five nights of sitting companionably together on the steps, Joe leaned over and took her hand, curling it inside his.

Margaret's oldest son had called from the hospital first thing on a Saturday morning at the end of September. She sat at the kitchen table drinking her tea while Ella spoke quietly into the phone for a few minutes. Ella hung up the phone and went to stand at the sink, her eyes fixed on the window that looked out over the backyard. She turned to Margaret and nodded.

"They say we should come and see him right away."

Margaret nodded in reply and pushed herself up and out of her chair, her hands gripping the table's edge. The ride to the hospital took place in slow motion. Margaret walked slowly and carefully along the hallway to Joe's room, holding her body erect. At his doorway, she paused and said a quick prayer to St. Ann for strength. Harry was sitting next to Joe's bed, leaning in to watch his father struggle for breath.

Margaret made her way to Joe's side and took his hands in hers.

"I'm here now, Joe," Margaret told him and Joe let out a rush of breath.

"I know," he said and tried to squeeze her hand.

"I'm here with you. You can go now," she said.

And he did.

By Christmas Margaret decided that she would join her husband. It started as a head cold that moved rapidly to her chest. Soon, her lungs felt heavy with fluid, and it was too much effort to take a breath. She lay in her bed, unwilling to get up. She accepted the occasional cup of tea from her daughter-in-law, a piece of toast. But, mostly, she slept. By the time Ella got wind of the situation, Margaret was ready to just close her eyes one last time and slip soundlessly away. But Ella arrived with an ambulance, and Margaret was carted off to the emergency room. She spent the next two weeks propped up on pillows in Ella's guest room, being coddled and jollied back to health.

*****

The nurses at the surgical ward are kind and they have doted on her since she arrived before supper. One of them was Ella's student in nursing school so she pays special attention to Margaret.

"How are you, Mrs. Kelly, my darling? Would you like a cup of tea and a few crackers?" she asked as soon as Margaret was settled in her room.

Margaret accepts the offers of an extra blanket and a softer pillow and smiles at the nurses as they smooth her hair and pat her hand. Her surgery is scheduled for the next morning. All of her children – the ones who still live in Newfoundland – and some of the grandchildren parade though her room all evening, bearing cards and flowers, potted plants and packages of chocolate. They lean in to kiss her soft cheek and hug her narrow shoulders. They are bright and cheery, praising the wonderful doctor who will perform the surgery and assuring her that she will be better than new once the nasty lump has been neatly snipped away. Margaret plays along with them, making them believe that all she wants is to be healthy and live another decade.

"That Dr. Furey is a prince. He'll take good care of me!"

One of the granddaughters has trouble keeping her brave face on and lets her eyes fill up, the tears spilling over cheeks, streaking the heavy eye makeup she insists on wearing. Margaret reaches out with a calloused thumb and wipes the girl's face.

"It's okay, Diane, sweetheart. I'll be fine no matter what! It just might be my time to go home!"

The others are thrown by this admission. They look at each other and do little to conceal their fear. She might be ninety, but none of them are ready for this.

"Now don't you be so foolish, Mom! You're not going any-where."

Her son, Tom, is getting red in the face. One of the daughters moves in to cluck over Margaret and clasp her hand.

"Of course not, Mom. We won't hear of it!"

Margaret is relieved when the last of them is ushered out of her room at 9:30 and the lights are dimmed to encourage sleep. The nurse asks if she'd like a little something just to relax her.

"It's a big day for you tomorrow. You're probably going to have a bit of trouble drifting off," she tells Margaret.

Margaret lets the tiny pill slide down her throat, chased with a gulp of water. She takes off her glasses and closes her eyes, which allows her to be with Joe. She remembers the first argument that she and Joe ever had after they were married. It was about money, Margaret recalls, but the details are indistinct. Joe was always big on paying cash for everything even if it meant waiting for months or years until they could afford something new for the house or the children. All Margaret can remember about that particular fight was that she had stomped out of the house and walked out the road, charging along the dirt shoulder until she wore herself out and had to come home. Joe was sitting on the back step, smoking his pipe, when she appeared in the laneway.

"You're not still mad at me, are you ducky?"

He tried to catch her hand as she passed him on the steps, but she shook him off. At the supper table, she refused to speak, sending messages down the table through the children to pass the potatoes or the fish. She sat staring sullenly into her plate after the meal was done, daring Joe to speak up first and apologize. A slice of soft white bread, cut from a golden loaf that she had baked that morning, came sailing down the table from Joe's end and smacked Margaret right between the eyes. She narrowed her eyes at Joe and gave him her blackest look, but he was laughing and, within seconds, so was she. They had a truce.

*****

The morning of the surgery comes in icy and dark. Grey light filters in through the window blinds, so thin that it barely registers on Margaret's eyes. She lies curled on her side on the hard hospital bed. This is the day that she will finally go home. It will be a relief from the loneliness and the ache in her side that started once Joe was no longer there.

On the way to the operating room, Ella is there, holding Margaret's hand. She gently removes Margaret's glasses and slips them into her pocket.

"I'll be there once you get out of surgery," Ella says and kisses her forehead.

Her daughter's face is the last thing Margaret sees. Before she slips under the anesthetic, Margaret can hear the operating room nurses and Dr. Furey chatting to her, promising that she will be ready for a game of cards and a few dances once they're done with her.

*****

The sounds buzzing around her head are dull, indistinguishable. Margaret opens her eyes but she can see little, only a haze of shapes. She peers into the fog, frantically searching for Joe. No sign of him.

"Joe? Joe? I'm here."

Margaret is scared by the panic in her own voice. She expected to feel calm and peaceful once she finally got here. But instead she is reaching out blindly, searching for something familiar and not finding it there.

"It's okay. You're okay!"

Ella's voice is clear and she takes Margaret's hand, holding it gently between both of hers.

Light Fingers

Philomena's mother is up to her elbows in bread dough when the phone rings. It's an old-fashioned phone, squat and black, with a stiff rotary dial. Philomena wishes they could get a modern phone, a coloured one with push buttons. The Flynns have a harvest gold wall phone in the kitchen of their split-level house in St. John's. It was one of the first things Philomena noticed when she went to work for Mrs. Flynn right after she finished Grade 11 back in June. Everything there is colour-coordinated. The kitchen is all done in harvest gold, right down to the canisters and the electric can opener. The bathroom has a mauve bathtub and toilet, and there are purple towels on all the racks. Even the soaps match.

"Are you going to look at that phone or are you going to answer it?" her mother says after the third ring. Philomena picks up the heavy receiver and says hello.

"Could I speak with your mother?" says the woman on the other end.

It's Mrs. Flynn. Her voice is crisp, precise, cold. Philomena does not say anything. She simply passes the phone to her mother and walks out the door.

*****

It's a quarter to two and the lunch crowd at Woolworth's has dribbled away. A few old men streel in for a bowl of soup, and the secretaries from up the street are here for a quick sandwich. Philomena pushes a grungy cloth in a lazy circle over the counter top.

She hauls off her hairnet and tries to fix her straggly pony tail. It's hard to feel beautiful when she's wearing a brown polyester uniform and a hairnet. It's one of the worst things about her new job. On her break, she sneaks to the bathroom to sponge the grease from her face with a damp wad of paper towels. She applies fresh makeup – a dab of creamy blusher, blended high on the round part of her cheeks, a slick of shiny lip gloss. She sniffs her underarms and sprays on some Love's Baby Soft, a cotton candy-smelling cologne that she got from the woman who runs the cosmetics counter. The bottle was a tester, the one the customers use to try out a new perfume. Winnie looks out for Philomena and gives her stuff that would only end up in the dumpster out back. Philomena treats it like it's Chanel Number 5.

She is talking to one of the old men, pouring him another cup of watery coffee, when she sees Miguel sail past the front window and into the store. She stops pouring for a second just to watch him move. He is not like the boys she grew up with around the bay. They came in two varieties – big, thick and stunned or small, sly and weasel-faced. But Miguel is like nothing else she's ever seen at home. He is soft-eyed, beautiful, exotic.

By the time he gets to the counter, Philomena has already poured a coffee for him and is cutting a slice of lemon meringue pie. He has tried all the pies that Woolworth's sells, and he says the lemon meringue is his "very most special favourite."

"Hello, Philly," Miguel says, as he slides onto one of the low stools at the counter and leans over the formica surface to look right into her face. Nobody calls her "Philly" but him. At home, the kids would shorten her name to Mena, which usually turned into Meanie. But Miguel says "Fee-lee" and it sounds beautiful, like a soap opera name. Philomena sighs his name as a form of greeting, and he gives her a smile that makes her catch her breath.

"Are you a very busy lady today?" Miguel asks. That's the thing with him. He's always asking about her. How is she feeling? Did she have a good morning? Do her feet hurt from standing up so much?

"Oh, I'm not doing too bad. I was nearly drove off my head at dinnertime. But now, it's slow," she says.

Miguel has been coming to visit her for over two weeks now. The first time, he was in the store with a crowd of Portuguese sailors, his fellow crewmembers. They were buying jeans, toys for their kids, presents for their wives. Miguel is only 21. He has no wife or children to shop for. So, while his friends searched the aisles for treasures, he sat at the counter and chatted with Philomena. Now he comes in every afternoon, telling her stories of Portugal, his family, his dreams to be captain of his own boat one day. But he doesn't hog the conversation. Miguel asks about Philomena and what she wants from life. It's the first time anyone has ever asked, and Philomena is embarrassed to realize that she does not have an answer.

Miguel is eating his pie, taking one small, neat bite after another.

"Mmm," he says, letting the meringue melt on his tongue. "You bake such a good pie, Philly."

She blushes at the compliment, even though it's not really hers. If only her mother could hear this! She says Philomena is so useless in the kitchen that she'll be lucky to ever get a husband.

"Thanks, Miguel," she says, any excuse to say his name, to let that melt on her tongue.

A gaggle of girls come into the store then and flounce past on their way to the home entertainment department. Philomena knows their routine. First, they look at the new 45's and giggle over their choices. Then, they go to the cosmetics department to smear on blue eye shadow and dip their baby fingers into pots of lip gloss. They wrap it up by sashaying out to the porch to get their photos taken in the coin-operated booth, screeching with laughter as they jockey for the best spot in front of the invisible camera before the flash goes off.

All of these girls look the same. They wear short, plaid bomber jackets with fake fur collars, which expose their skinny bums and reedy thighs. Their hair is long and shiny, thanks to endless bottles of shampoo and creme rinse, parted in the middle and flipped back with the help of a curling iron. Philomena is thinking about buying a curling iron for herself. It would force her to give up something this week. But, if it would make her look better, she'd make the sacrifice. She feels a flutter of resentment towards these girls, who have everything they want and don't even know it. They live in newly constructed bungalows and split-level houses in the east end. Philomena knows because they are just like the kids she used to babysit. The Flynns have two girls – ten and twelve. They each have their own room, with Shaun Cassidy and Leif Garrett posters on the walls. They gather with their friends in the family room to watch TV and play records. They take turns doing each other's hair and makeup, trying to make themselves look like teenagers instead of girls.

Philomena longs for nice things. It's not that she's greedy. She just wants something of her own, straight from the store. A tiny gold heart on a chain, a long coat that flares out on the bottom, a pair of jeans – girl's jeans, with a flower embroidered on the pocket, not ones passed down from her brothers. That hunger got worse when she worked for the Flynns. Every day she was surrounded by things she wanted, and seeing them made her desperate, even reckless. It started small. She pocketed a perfumed guest soap from the tiny bathroom off the front hallway. Then she would slide her hand over the pile of loose change on Mr. Flynn's bureau. Eventually, Philomena found herself sitting in front of the dresser in Debbie's room and admiring her jewellery box, filled with cheap, beautiful necklaces and earrings.

Miguel has finished his pie, running the edge of his fork along the plate to catch the last of the lemon filling.

"Thank you very much, Philly," he says, pushing the plate to one side.

Philomena smiles at him and fills his coffee cup for the third time. Her boss would give her a hard look if he saw that.

"I have a question I am wanting to ask you," Miguel says, dipping his head slightly and looking up at her through a fringe of dark hair.

She gives him a warm smile, what she hopes is an encouraging smile.

"I would like to take you to the movie show at the Paramount Theatre," he says, earnestly extending his invitation.

"That would be very nice, Miguel," Philomena replies quickly, before he can change his mind.

They make plans for the next evening, both of them eager to make it official. He will meet her at her boarding house on

Bond Street, and they will walk to the movie theatre. Miguel touches her hand, a sweet, cautious gesture.

"You are making me very happy, Philly," he tells her before he slides the money for his pie and coffee across the counter and gets up to leave.

When her shift is over, Philomena makes a stop in the cosmetics department and sizes up the curling irons. There is one on sale for $5.99, one that features a tiny dot on the handle that changes colour when it has reached the right temperature. She knows how it works. Debbie and Tina Flynn each had one just like this sitting on the ornate, white dressers in their bedrooms. When they were at school, she would experiment with new hairstyles and try to copy the ones she saw in the girls' teen magazines. She wonders sometimes which one of them tattled on her. How did they even notice the few things missing from their bedrooms? They had so much. She had taken things carefully, one item every few weeks, storing them in a shopping bag in her bedroom closet in the Flynns' basement. A necklace, a hair clip, a red transistor radio. It was as if each thing had found its way into her hand, and once she was holding it, she couldn't let go, clutching it to her chest as she raced to her room to hide her treasure. It hurt to give everything back. She felt a real physical pain as her mother grabbed the bag from her hands and wrenched it away.

Philomena shakes her head to dislodge that memory and thinks instead about sitting in the darkness with Miguel at the Paramount, his hand laid gently over hers on the armrest, his shoulder touching hers. She closes her eyes and imagines him stroking her hair, hair that's been transformed into silky coils by the curling iron. Maybe he will whisper into her ear and tell her how pretty she looks tonight, how nice she smells, how soft her hair feels.

"Are you going to buy that or are you just going to drool over it?"

She whips her head around to see Derek King, one of the young guys from the sports department. He normally towers over her head, but he has stooped to speak directly into her ear. She turns so quickly that her cheekbone smacks into his chin, causing them both to clutch their faces in pain.

"Oooh, you're a dangerous one," he says.

But he is laughing, and that makes Philomena smile, too, forgetting for a moment that she is usually dumbstruck around Derek. This is the kind of guy that the Flynn girls will have as their boyfriends when they get to high school. He lives in the suburbs with his parents and two brothers, drives a brand-new yellow Pinto and spends his days at the Trades College, where he takes the Electronics Tech course. Woolworth's is just a pit stop on the way to his real life, a place he works part-time to help pay for his car. He has never spoken to Philomena before, other than a curt greeting when they happen to be punching their time cards at the same moment.

"So whatcha doing? Getting ready for a big date?" he teases her.

Derek is never at a loss for a date. Girls are always trailing into the store to say hi while he's on his break. They stand and look up at him with worshipping gazes, taking in his hockey player build and long hair, cut short at the front and sides. Philomena finds herself turning into one of those girls on the spot, giving Derek a coy smile, delighted that he's even interested in her after-work activities. He leans in close to her face again and lowers his voice.

"But please tell me you're not going out with one of the Portuguese," he whispers, and his breath on her ear makes her face grow hot.

"What?" she mumbles. "What do you mean?"

Derek stands back then and assumes his normal stance, pulling his long torso up and his wide shoulders back. His expression is not friendly anymore.

"I mean, the only girls who go with the Portuguese are the whores. Don't you know that? Haven't you ever heard of the girls who go down to the boats?"

Philomena looks at her feet, wishing he would walk away now, wishing she could get away from him without ever having to lift her eyes. She feels red-hot shame creeping up her neck on its way to her face, leaving bright, mottled patches on her pale skin. She knows the feeling of being caught. This is just how she felt the day Mrs. Flynn called her mother.

"No, I don't know about those girls," she says.

"Well, then, let me tell you all about it," Derek says, speaking to her as if she is simple. "They go to bars with the Portuguese and get drunk, and then they go back to the boats. They take money from the Portuguese, and then they lie down and open their legs for them."

Philomena steps back from him then, one hand to her mouth as if he had reached out and smacked her across the face. She can't imagine why he's saying this to her. She wonders for a moment if this is a joke, if he will throw back his head and laugh, poking her in the sides and making her laugh, too. The laughter would be such a relief.

"So come on, Philomena," he says, stepping into the silence and filling it with another hoarse whisper. "Please tell me you're not going out with one of the Portuguese."

"No," she says. "Don't be so foolish."

Derek grins at her and chucks her under the chin as if she was a child.

"I knew you were a smart girl," he says.

"I have to go now," she tells him.

Philomena calls goodbye to Derek over her shoulder as she walks towards the door. Her voice makes a thin sound that disappears into the air. She pushes the glass door open and walks out onto the sidewalk. She walks two blocks on Water Street before she looks down and sees that the curling iron is still in her hand. Philomena does not hesitate before she opens the crumpled Woolworth's bag that holds her dirty uniform and puts the long, narrow box inside. Then she heads for Bowring's.

As soon as she walks in the door, she knows she's in a different world, one where the scent of real perfume hangs in the air instead of the grease from the cafeteria. Instrumental music murmurs to her from unseen stereo speakers. No one is screeching on the intercom, paging the stock boys to come with a trolley. On the main floor, she examines the glass shelves that display dozens of hats and gloves, and matching scarves. She has been eyeing a tam made of pale pink angora wool, a hat that costs more than the winter jacket she bought on sale at Woolworth's before Christmas. Her hand darts out to touch it, to smooth its silky hair. It curls around her hand like a kitten, and with one swift move she scrunches it into a ball and presses it into the bag under her arm.

The next afternoon, Miguel comes in a bit later than usual. Philomena has been watching the clock since one, wondering what she will say when she sees him. He slips onto one of the stools while her back is turned, and she jumps when she sees his face, beaming at her.

"Hello, Philly. I could not wait for tonight," he says, reaching for her hand.

But she pulls it back, jamming both of her hands into the pockets of her uniform. Miguel looks bewildered.

"I don't think I can go out with you," she tells him.

"What is wrong? Are you unhappy with me?" he asks.

Philomena folds her arms firmly across her chest, trying to look stern. She turns away from Miguel's crumpled face for a second, ashamed that she's the one who is making him look so sad. She sees Derek King watching her from his post in the sporting goods department. He's leaning on a pile of boxes, staring a straight line across the store that burrows right into her forehead. She looks down and closes her eyes, blotting out both of their faces. When she looks up again, Miguel is leaning towards her over the counter.

"What is wrong?" he repeats.

Philomena opens her mouth, and the words spill out before she's even planned what to say.

"I can't go. I just can't. I should never have said yes in the first place," she says.

Miguel stares at her, and he looks so surprised that she instantly regrets saying anything. She has made a mistake. Maybe Derek was wrong after all.

"Why? Why do you say this?" Miguel asks.

"Because, we are different. We have no business being with each other," she says, but she sounds stupid, as if the teacher had called on her and she didn't know the answer, so she started making one up.

"No business? What do you mean 'business'?" he asks.

Philomena looks at her feet, studying the scuffed toes of her sensible work shoes. She wishes Miguel would stop asking her questions that she can't answer. Finally, he obliges. He stands up and takes a package out of his pocket, a tiny, black box with a pink ribbon tied around it.

"For you, Philly. It is a gift for you. Just for you," he says.

Philomena holds the box in her hand and watches him leave. It is from Silver's Jewellery across the street. She has spent many an afternoon in there, peering into the display cases that line the walls, pressing her nose to the glass to get a closer look at the earrings, the necklaces, the beautiful glittery pieces made from silver and gold, with stones set in them. Derek is still watching her, so she slips the box into her pocket and starts wiping down the counters.

Her shift goes on forever. At five o'clock, Philomena changes her clothes, punches her time card in the heavy metal clock and shrugs on her coat. The box from Silver's Jewellery is carefully nestled at the bottom of her Woolworth's bag. She clutches the bag close as she leaves the store. Down the street at Shelley's Restaurant, Philomena orders a Pepsi and a plate of chips, which will allow her to sit in the front window for at least half an hour. She uses her paper napkin to polish a spot on the table in front of her until it gleams. She takes the box out of her bag and lays it on the newly shined spot. It sits there almost vibrating, with an energy that begs her to open it. But she waits, eating her chips one by one, dipping the tip of each one in a puddle of ketchup. She drinks the Pepsi slowly, savouring each mouthful. Twenty minutes pass before she wipes her fingertips clean with her napkin and unties the ribbon. She lifts the top off and opens the folded tissue paper, pulling out a fine gold chain with a wafer-thin heart dangling from it. She holds it up to the light that filters in from the street lamp and sees minuscule ornate script engraved on one side. *Philly.* She rubs the smooth piece of gold between her finger and thumb, stares at her new name etched in gold.

The morning that Mrs. Flynn called her mother, Philomena ran from the house without even putting on her coat. She walked down to the wharf and sat there in the cool, damp breeze, trying to come up with answers for her mother, for the questions she would inevitably shriek at her. No, she didn't know what she thought she was doing. No, she didn't think about what Mrs. Flynn was going to do when she found out. Yes, she knew she would have to find herself another job and a place to live when she went back to town on Monday. Yes, she knew very well that she was an ungrateful girl who didn't deserve the opportunity the Flynns had given her.

Philomena leaves the restaurant and steps outside into the cold evening again, walking towards the waterfront. She isn't sure which boat is Miguel's, but she scans the name on the bow of each one, looking for something that sounds familiar. About a dozen men are playing soccer on the harbour apron, running and panting, their breath puffing out in front of them in wispy clouds. They are laughing and calling to one another in Portuguese as they kick the ball and dart around each other. But the action slows to a crawl when Philomena stops walking and peers at their faces in the dim light.

"Hello there, beautiful lady," one of the sailors calls and does an exaggerated swagger as he walks toward her. "I am the man you want!"

The others laugh and poke each other in the sides with their elbows. A voice calls out something in Portuguese that makes them all stop. A man is standing on the deck of one of the boats, looking down at the soccer game and at Philomena.

"Are you looking for someone?" he calls to her, and his voice is kind.

Philomena tilts her head back and peers up at the man's face.

"Miguel. I'm looking for Miguel," she calls up to him.

"Sorry," he says, shaking his head sadly. "He's not here."

Distance

The volunteers have set up a command post in an empty storefront on a busy street that runs through the neighbourhood. Ever since it opened, people have spilled through the doors, anxious to do something. A handful of high school students make posters and flyers with Tyler's face on them; another group takes them out to post on telephone poles and windows. Daisy, a retired nurse, is on duty at the phone. She listens carefully to every caller before she decides if it's a legitimate lead or simply another call from an attention-seeking crackpot.

"Well, thank you for your help," Daisy says politely into the receiver, rolling her eyes in Anita's direction.

Anita sits on a plastic chair with her tape recorder and notepad on her knees. She nods at Daisy and raises her eyebrows in commiseration. Back at the newsroom, they have been getting the same kinds of calls. There are the people who are sure that the guy down the hall has abducted Tyler or that the old man who plays chess in the park has the little boy hidden away back in his boarding house. A woman with psychic powers calls to say she can feel Tyler's presence behind a shopping mall in Richmond Hill. The next time, she can see him in a cottage on Lake Huron. Anita has been on the story ever since the day that Tyler was reported missing so she has heard it all.

Daisy hangs up the phone and turns to Anita.

"Sorry to keep you waiting, honey. That phone never stops." She shakes her head.

"No problem," says Anita.

She likes Daisy. She's a sensible woman who simply wants to help – unlike some of the bizarre characters who have taken to hanging around the command post. A crisis seems to draw in the people from the edges, the ones who never get a chance to take part in anything else. In a few short weeks, a complicated dynamic has developed within the group of volunteers. Alliances have been formed, friendships tested, conspiracies weaved. The competition is fierce among those who want to be one of the insiders, one of the people who really know what's going on. Anita got sucked in by a couple of the fringe people early on, a couple of guys who led her off on a futile expedition to find a guy with a great story about seeing Tyler the night before. These days, she turns to Daisy to find out who to trust for good information and who to ignore.

"He left you a message," Daisy says. "Meet him around the corner at the coffee shop. Away from all of the big ears!"

Anita laughs and gathers her stuff.

"Thanks, Daisy. Hope tonight's a good one."

Outside, it's hot and the rain has started again, a whisper of mist that has been floating to the ground off and on for the last few days. Nothing dries in this weather. Anita gets out of the shower every morning and rubs her hair with a towel. But the water never evaporates. Her hair hangs in damp curls at her neck and around her face.

The windows of the coffee shop are steamy. Anita sits at a table and traces patterns on the foggy glass. It is much too hot to be drinking this metallic coffee, with beads of oil from the fake cream bobbing on the surface.

After almost twenty minutes have passed, Tony comes in the door and looks around for her. He's tall and sturdy. He works outdoors – he's in construction. His face and neck and arms are brown, and his shaggy hair has been streaked by the sun. Blue-black bruises underline his eyes. He hasn't slept much lately. It's been 19 days since his son disappeared. He catches a few restless hours of sleep just before the sun comes up. He doesn't want to waste any precious hours of daylight in bed, when he could be out looking for his boy. He sees Anita and comes over to sit down.

"Hi," he says, his eyes darting around the room.

"How are you doing?"

"Me?" he says. "I'm okay. So, do you have anything?"

She stalls him, asks if he wants a coffee.

"No, no."

Tony wants her to get on with it. She's developed some connections at the police station during her first year on the crime beat. He's sure that they know something, and he is convinced that Anita can find out what it is. She is afraid to tell him that she's hit a wall with the police, the guys on the case. They won't give her anything else. Mostly, they're afraid it will turn up in the paper, and the chief will know who gave her the information.

"No," she says carefully. "Nothing new."

"Ah, shit," he says.

He's trying to look calm, as if he never really expected her to have anything.

"I'm running out of time," he says. "The longer he's gone, the harder it's going to be to find him."

The longer he's gone, the less likely it is that he's alive. Anita knows that just from reviewing the coverage of other missing children's cases. She tries to lead Tony to that conclusion on his own, gently steering him in that direction, calmly toning down his optimism. But he never wavers.

Anita feels her face grow hotter. Then she feels a cool sweat bead on her forehead. She cups her hand over her mouth. She could throw up the bitter coffee or just faint to the floor. Instead, she closes her eyes and imagines the cool tile against her cheek. The nausea passes.

"How did the search go today?" Anita says to him, steering him back to the practical.

"What?" he says, as if he can't quite understand her.

"You searched the ravine today. How did it go?"

He's restless now, distracted, even a little irritated that he's come here for nothing.

"It went okay," he says. "But we didn't find anything."

She reaches past the metal napkin dispenser and the glass sugar canister and puts her hand on his forearm. Her palm is warm and sticky on his cool, dry skin.

"I'm sorry," she says.

"Let's go outside," he says, standing up. "It's got to be cooler out there."

It's still raining, heavier now. They walk through a crush of people on the sidewalk and down the street. He turns the corner onto a street lined with houses. It is shrouded in a canopy of leafy trees. The rain patters through the branches, making soft slapping sounds.

"Was Ellen there today?" she asks him.

Ellen is his wife. But they've been separated for almost five months. Tyler went missing on a day he was with Tony. Ellen never comes out and says it's his fault, but she looks at him with gritted teeth. She has shrivelled in the past 19 days, the flesh melting from her body, leaving the tendons in her neck exposed and taut. She does not eat, but her doctor feeds her a steady stream of tranquilizers. Anita wonders if that's why she seems so distant and removed from the drama that is her life these days.

"No, Ellen didn't come today," Tony says. "She's not feeling too good."

"That's too bad."

She never knows quite what to say to him. Every word falls out of her mouth and lands impotently on the ground. She can't offer him any hope, and she can't console him. The hardest part is stopping herself from saying there's no point in searching any more. So she doesn't say anything.

The next day, Anita convinces her editor that she should join the searchers as they comb through an area just outside the city. The search is based on a tip received by an officer at one of the smaller regional police forces. Dan, who's on the assignment desk this morning, is skeptical.

"Come on, Anita. Someone is just yanking this poor guy's chain. What are the odds that you'll find anything out there today?"

He leans back on his chair, rocking slowly as he watches Anita's face.

"I don't know. This could be something. The leads come from the strangest places!"

Dan shakes his head.

"Anita, you have yourself too wrapped up in this case."

"I'll just go on this search. Just this one," Anita says, like a kid begging to stay up late.

Dan uses his feet to roll his chair closer to Anita. He lowers his voice to grab her full attention.

"Okay. But it has to stop after this. You can't be a member of the team."

*****

The phone rings in the middle of the night. It is Tony on the line, but it's hard to understand anything he's saying.

135

"What's wrong?" Anita asks.

He is crying into the phone.

"I had a dream that he is floating in the water. He's wearing his T-shirt with Mickey Mouse on the front. His face is in the water."

He moans in a low, rumbling way.

"Oh, Tony, I'm so sorry. What can I do?" she asks him.

Anita tells him she'll be right there. She gets out of bed and pulls her damp T-shirt over her head on her way to the bathroom. In the shower, she bends down and turns back the hot water faucet until the water runs down her back in cool waves.

If people at the paper knew what she was doing tonight, she'd be dragged into the city editor's office the first thing in the morning. He'd have a serious little talk with her about keeping her emotional distance from her stories. Anita made the editors nervous. On the one hand, she was the best person to send when someone had been murdered or killed in a horrific accident. She could get any grieving family to talk. She always got the best family photos of the victim and the most poignant anecdotes. But she would always cry with them and hug them when she left, and they would call her for days and weeks afterwards, just to talk. The editors thought she got too involved.

It is too late to safely take the street car. So Anita gets dressed and calls a cab. Tony lives in a tiny house on the other side of the Don Valley. She's been there dozens of times in the last few weeks to do interviews or to accompany Tony and the volunteers on a search. It is a neighbourhood where people have lived for a couple of generations. Tony's house belonged to his father and mother. He's the youngest of nine children, so his parents are old now and live in a seniors' complex in Scarborough. Anita walks up the front lane and knocks on the screen door. The inside door is open, and she can see Tony sitting on the couch, his forehead resting on his palms.

She goes inside and kneels on the floor in front of him, peeling his hands away from his face.

"It's okay," she says to him.

He peers at her, through eyes that are nearly swollen shut.

"I saw him," he says. "He's dead."

Anita puts her arms around him. He slides off the couch to the floor and curls into her, his face pressed into her breasts, his arms around her waist. She rocks him like that for a while, runs the back of her hand against his cheek.

"You should try again to get some sleep," Anita says to him.

"I can't," he says. "I don't want to see him any more."

"It's okay," she says. "I'll be here."

She disentangles him from her body and stands up, pulling him up with her. They walk to the bedroom, him leaning heavily on her shoulder. He towers over her. It's hard for her to hold him up. He sits on the edge of the bed while she turns on the fan, opens a window.

"Lie down," she says.

Anita walks around to the other side of the bed and lies next to him. They lie on their backs and look up at the ceiling. He takes her hand and holds it tightly, crushing her ring against her finger.

Tony sobs quietly as he slips into an uneasy sleep. He shudders and grabs for her frantically. Once his arm is around her, he drifts back to sleep. She eventually falls asleep, too, with his breath at her ear. She dreams about Tyler running behind her on a crowded street, his small body darting in and around the legs of the adults.

Anita wakes up when the sun creeps into the room. It's six-fifteen. Her shift doesn't start until three o'clock today. Tony opens his eyes. She can feel his lashes bat against her neck. He runs his hand along her arm, back and forth. He traces her elbow with his finger. She's wearing a cotton dress, but it's tangled around her legs. He pushes the fabric up along her thigh and slides his hand down her leg. She stares at the wall. She doesn't stop him. He pulls off his clothes and unbuttons her dress. They lie together, their skin touching, for a long time. He kisses her neck and holds onto her so tightly that she holds her breath.

Around noon, she takes a shower in his bathroom and washes her hair with his shampoo. He makes her breakfast. They drink a pot of tea on the back porch, sheltered from the sun. They've barely spoken since they opened their eyes. Tony looks out at the garden and says Ellen never wanted to have a child.

"She says she didn't know if she'd figure out how to love one. I told her I'd show her. There was nothing to it."

Anita goes to work, wearing the wrinkled dress she slept in. Her editor sends her to a news conference at city hall, and she's relieved that she doesn't have to think any more. She files her story early and sits around drinking coffee with a couple of the copy editors. One of the summer reporters comes running out of the radio room, where he's been listening to all the police scanners.

"They've found a body in the lake," he says. "Down in the east end."

Anita is calm.

"I'll go," she says. She picks up her knapsack and her cell phone and calls a cab.

When the cab driver drops her at the wharf, Anita looks for a gaggle of reporters. But there's just one guy there from the wire service. The others mustn't have had their radios on. He is scribbling in his notebook when she walks up to him.

"Hi," he says. "I guess you've heard that it's the little boy."

"Yeah," Anita says. "Has his father been down yet?"

"Just left," the guy says. "The police took him up to the station. They'll have a news conference at ten o'clock."

Anita walks over to the edge of the wharf. The cops are zipping Tyler into a body bag. The photographer from Anita's paper must have gotten here just before her because he's snapping pictures from over the fence with a zoom lens. Anita looks down into the murky water. Bits of garbage cling to the edge of the dock. She uses her cell phone to call another cab. On the way to the police station, she dictates the beginning of her story to one of the editors over the phone. When she gets to the station, the lobby is alive with reporters and TV cameras. She peers through the bright lights to see if Tony is there yet.

Just after ten, the lead investigator on Tyler's case walks into the lobby, with Tony and Ellen behind him. Anita joins the rush as people scramble for a good spot right up front. The cop announces what everyone knows already. A three-year-old boy was found floating in the lake. His parents have identified him as the child who disappeared almost three weeks ago. Ellen is crying quietly. Tony has his arms around her. He's smoothing her hair in a slow, steady way. He is not crying. Ellen presses her face into his white cotton shirt, leaving a wet spot that spreads. The cop says they are looking for a suspect in the murder. Ellen cries out sharply then, and Tony pulls her closer. Anita writes it all down in her notebook.

Only I Can Make Me Happy

The clerk at the Queen Elizabeth Hotel in Montreal calls to say there's a problem with our reservation. It seems the honeymoon suite was already booked. Someone made a mistake when they promised me the room.

"Terribly sorry," he says.

I thank him and hang up. Maybe the best thing I can do is simply call off the wedding. It doesn't really seem fair, I know, because it was all my idea.

*****

Lily told me on our second date that her family was not very good at marriage.

"There are eight Mrs. Martins. But there are only four brothers," Lily said, ticking them off on her fingers. "One wife for Uncle John, two for Dad, two for Harry and three for Stan."

Lily has a family tale that she can use to get herself out of most dilemmas. Once, I happened to mention that her constant lateness was a bit annoying. She folded her bottom lip in under her top teeth and turned her face away from me. After a few minutes of silence, she looked back at me, all big eyes and pouty mouth.

"I'm sorry, darling," she began. "It's just I'm so afraid to show up and find you're not there. I'd rather come late and be sure you'll be waiting."

I knew what was coming next. Lily launched into a sorrowful story of the dad who could not be counted on to do anything he promised. Her eyes fixed on a spot just to the left of my chin, Lily recounted how she had often waited by herself in the school parking lot. She watched as the other parents pulled up in their station wagons and Pintos and collected little bunches of chattering children. The teachers' cars slowly disappeared from the parking spaces; the teachers themselves stopping by first to see if she needed a ride.

"No," Lily told them. "My Dad's coming for me."

By five o'clock, she had done her homework, sitting on the cement curb with her books propped on her knees. It was getting dark. The night cleaning crew arrived in their grey van, carting buckets and mops into the school.

"What are you doing here all by yourself, ducky?" one of the men said.

"My Dad's coming," she told him.

It was close to 6:30 when her father's royal blue Torino sailed into the parking lot and glided to a stop in front of her. He leaned across the wide plush seat and flung the passenger door open. Cigarette smoke and the theme music from the CBC evening news swirled out into the cold evening air.

"I'm sorry, baby," he said. "I was in a meeting, and I just forgot all about you."

Lily gathered her books and fitted them back into her brown leather school bag. She slowly buckled it up and looked up at her father.

"That's okay, Daddy."

By the time Lily finishes a story like that, I am beaten. What can I say? Only a heartless bastard could sit there without a tear hanging in the corner of one eye. And I, it seems, am not one of them. So, I put my arms around her narrow shoulders and hold her close, smoothing her hair with my open palm.

"I'm sorry, baby," I tell her.

I thought things would change once I moved into her doll-sized house, wedged into a tiny lane off a downtown street. I have to duck and stoop to get through the doorways. I am always banging into tables and bookcases, jarring plants and unsettling stacks of books. My footsteps make the pewter picture frames, glass candle holders and clay pots tremble and teeter near the edges.

There are only four rooms, so it is easy to be together. It seems to me that we are always connected by a string of touches or breaths or words. If she is lying in the bath, I can talk to her from the living room without even raising my voice. We almost have to embrace to pass one another in the narrow hallway. Our knees bump under the small glass table in the kitchen.

But when Lily lies curled around me at night, her silky foot tracing the sole of mine, my hand cradling her fingers, she still sighs into the darkness.

"I feel so alone."

In the beginning, I found it impossible to console Lily. My arms hung at my sides, limp and useless. My lips moved, forming words that sounded stupid and insincere as soon as they floated out of my mouth. I would look down at her as she cried, and wonder where all those tears came from. She seemed to have an inexhaustible supply, a water conservation area of her very own.

"I wish I could do something to make you happy," I used to say.

Lily would turn to me, resigned and weary.

"Only I can make me happy."

But that is not exactly true. When I come home with her favourite flavour of Haagen Daaz ice cream, one that's carried by only two stores in the entire city, Lily is incredulous but happy. She cannot believe that I would take a bus to another part of town just to buy her a treat.

"But you don't even like this kind!" Lily said, the first time I presented her with the icy carton, my fingerprints melted into the cloudy surface.

"I know. It's for you."

She cried (happy tears, she assured me) and got herself a spoon. After that, I realized that it was not the size of the gesture. It was the act of thinking about her that made Lily happy. I took to calling her at the bookstore, at times when I knew business was slow.

"Hello?" she said cautiously, the first time the other clerk handed her the phone.

"Hey baby, it's me."

"Hal! Is something wrong?"

I could see her face, eyes narrowed in worry.

"No, everything's perfect. I just wanted to say hi and see how your day is going."

There was silence, then the ring of the cash register behind her; and, finally, a sigh, her breath rushing into my ear.

"Thank you."

This was evidence that I loved her. Documentation. Something she could consider as she lay in bed at night and wondered if she were still alone. At the very least, Lily knew I was thinking about her, that I had not forgotten her in the hours we were separated each day. It was so easy to make her happy that it seemed mean not to bother.

*****

I got to thinking about marriage just a couple of weeks ago. We were planning our first trip together — a week in Montreal in July. Lily has a friend from university who lives right downtown.

"We could stay with her. She'd love to meet you," Lily said.

"There's a park at the foot of the mountain where the African drummers play all day," she said, with a shiver of anticipation. "I can close my eyes now and hear that sound roll right over me."

"And I want to go to my favourite bar in Sylvie's neighbourhood, where they aren't supposed to sell liquor unless there's food on the table."

She told me about the dishes of shiny black olives that sit on the tables for days, their slick, dark skins eventually growing dry and dull. Lily got excited and started making lists of places we had to visit and exhibitions we had to see. There were restaurants on Prince Arthur, little bistros where they encouraged you to bring your own wine.

Her happiness was fleeting and effervescent. It bubbled under my nose. Made me laugh. Made me brave.

"You know what, baby?" I said to her as she filled pages of blank paper with lists.

"I always thought the best way to get married would be to elope."

Her pen stopped, hovered over the page.

"Just go away on a trip. Visit City Hall and come home and tell everyone we got married," I said.

Lily looked at me, waiting for the punchline.

"What do you say? Let's get married in Montreal."

She picked up the loose pages and stacked them neatly, evening the edges by tapping them sharply on the table top. She looked at me, plucked a blank sheet from the pile of paper and wrote "Wedding" across the top.

"Only if you're sure," she said finally.

"Absolutely positive," I said.

"Okay," she said, and started making a new list. Wedding licence. Dress. Rings.

Two hours later, I gathered some papers and files and slunk out of the house.

"I need to do some work at the office," I lied to Lily.

"I'll miss you," she said, pressing her lips to my face, rubbing the words into my skin.

I went for coffee, instead, and took two hours to read the Saturday *Globe*, scouring every article, every ad. Finally, I just sat there and studied the beads of oil floating on the surface of my coffee.

Now, I'd gone and done it. This had gone beyond bringing home ice cream and candles that smelled of lavender and glass bottles of bath salts. This was much more serious than birthday and Valentine's cards that solemnly intoned *I love you so very much*. I had made the big gesture, the one that was supposed to make Lily happy and secure.

She once asked me about Elaine, my ex, the woman who had left me more than a year ago.

"Elaine is athletic," I told her. "She plays volleyball and tennis. She hikes on the weekends. She works in the Finance Department with the province. She's an analyst of some kind. What else do you want to know?"

"What does she look like?"

"Tall. Short blonde hair. She's kind of boyish."

Lily looked down at her miniature hands and the sombre floral dress hanging around her ankles, fingered a long curl of dark red hair.

"I don't suppose she was clingy like me," Lily said.

"Elaine is very independent," I told her.

I did not say: Elaine is so independent that she didn't need me at all. She wedged me into her schedule, fitted me in among sports tournaments, committee meetings and week-end adventure treks. And sometimes, she just couldn't fit me in.

"But I love you more than I ever loved Elaine," I said, taking a final, fearless leap.

Lily lifted her eyebrows, an exaggerated declaration of doubt. Really? her face said to me.

*****

Lily called Sylvie to tell her about the latest development in her life, and they were on the phone for an hour, chattering in French and English, Lily's voice bobbing up and down like a little boat riding choppy seas. Her laughter spilled out into the hallway, deep chuckles and hoots of delight that I had never heard from Lily before. I sat in the living room, trying to read, but I was distracted by the snippets of conversation I could hear and intrigued by the bits I couldn't. For example, I wondered what provoked Lily to say in a high, tremulous voice: Well, of course I want to get married!

I turned my eyes back to my magazine when I heard the phone receiver clatter back into its cradle and then Lily's light step on the stairs. She appeared in the doorway and waited for me to look up. Finally, I did.

"So, how's Sylvie?" I inquired blandly.

"Sylvie? Oh, she's wonderful. She's very excited for us!"

Lily perched on the coffee table, propped her elbows on her knees and planted her chin in her hands.

"We came up with a lovely plan," she told me, building me up for whatever announcement she was about to make.

It's something about the wedding, I figured. Sylvie had decided to throw us a big party, a reception after the ceremony at the courthouse.

"I'm going to fly to Montreal a week early and spend some time with Sylvie. Maybe visit with some of my old friends."

I looked at Lily, bewildered.

"You mean you're going to leave a week before me?" I asked.

Her brow crumpled.

"That's okay with you, isn't it?"

"Sure," I said. "Well, I guess."

"Excellent," Lily said and slapped her thighs with her hands. She stood up briskly.

"Excellent," she repeated.

*****

The first day after Lily leaves, I make a series of calls to hotels around Montreal, searching for the perfect room for our wedding night. I finally find one in a rustic, old inn just outside the city – a honeymoon suite that includes a clawfoot bathtub and a fireplace. Lily will love it.

In her absence, I handle the household chores. I cut my finger on the ragged edge of a tin can while I'm bagging the recycling. I do not heal well. My hands and arms are marked with white scars. An accident with an axe ripped off the top of my index finger when I was thirteen. I still remember the feeling of blade striking bone. A small oval of skin was neatly snipped from my inner arm to cover the gaping tip of my finger. I can feel the tiny ridges left by the stitches in both spots. But my skin also remembers less serious wounds. A giggling girlfriend from my university days had clawed at my arm with her finger nails when I tickled her mercilessly. The scars look like they were created by small, sharp blades.

Lily's skin looks delicate, but it is remarkably resilient. She fell down a craggy embankment one afternoon when we were hiking. The hike was my idea. Instead of rolling into the fall, Lily fought it all the way, her small hands grabbing at rocks and tree branches as her body hurtled past. She was not crying when I scrabbled down the bank to get to her. She sat there bleeding from her numerous scrapes and cuts and carefully picked out the bits of gravel that were embedded in her skin. The worst gash left a crescent-shaped mark on the skin around her knee cap. But within a week it turned pink and showed signs of healing. It barely left a mark.

The second day she's gone, I check the stereo to see if Lily left a CD in the player, something she'd been listening to recently. I press the button to start the music and wait for the whoosh that the CD makes as it starts to spin. Nothing.

Lily's miniature house grows in height and width and depth while she is away. I feel empty spaces eddying around me as I walk from room to room.

By the third night, I find it hard to sleep. Usually, Lily is asleep before I get to bed, her body staking a claim on the mattress. Her head is in one corner, and her feet are stretched into the opposite corner at the end of the bed. I gently move her limbs to make space for myself, but as soon as I've curled onto one side, her arms and legs migrate back to their original positions regardless of what's in their way. I always think I will revel in the space that an empty bed offers me, but when I find myself lying there alone, I end up curled into the same old position.

*****

I hail a cab at Dorval Airport and tell the driver that I'm going to the Plateau. He slows down and starts counting off the street numbers on Laval Street . . . 1176, 1178, 1180. I lean out the window when I catch sight of Lily on the sidewalk up ahead.

Sylvie is standing on the front step behind Lily, a small boy perched on her hip. She's a tall woman with a severe black bob, straight bangs fringing her eyes. I pay the cabbie, collect my bags and head for Lily. Sylvie looks over at me, a stare that lasts entirely too long. A look of appraisal and, I sense immediately, disapproval.

"Hello, darling," Lily says, giving me a sweet kiss.

"Well, hello, Hal. Finally, we meet," Sylvie says, extending her hand.

"Yes," I say. "Finally."

We go inside, the little boy, Andre, leading the way, pulling his mother by the hand. The house is old, but it's been recently restored. Exposed beams, pine floors, a big stove in the middle of the living room. Lily takes my arm and walks me through the house, pointing out renovations that Sylvie has done recently. I nod at the spacious living room and kitchen, murmur approval at the stained-glass window retrieved from the ruins of an old church in northern Quebec.

Sylvie suggests that I must be tired, and Lily turns to me in surprise, as if she's forgotten that I have not been here with her all along.

"Of course, Hal, you must be totally exhausted," she exclaims, and leads me upstairs to our room.

While I unpack my bag and unfold clothes, Lily buzzes around me, hands flying. She hangs shirts on wooden hangers and smoothes the wrinkles with busy fingers. She is full of stories of the adventures she's been on so far. Bike rides, hikes, picnics, concerts. When all of my things are neatly stored away, I turn to Lily and fold her into my arms.

"I missed you," I tell her.

"Mmm, me too," she says and kisses me with uncharacteristic fervour.

That evening, we have a barbeque out in the backyard. Sylvie has invited some old friends over, people that Lily knows from university days, people she worked with on Amnesty International campaigns and at the campus radio station. Eva, Mark, Claude, Nancy, Charlie – they arrive together, weighed down with bottles of wine, brown paper packages from the butcher, a bowl of salad.

Andre is allowed to stay up for the party. He tails Lily, hangs off her legs, crawls into her lap every time she sits down. She talks to him in a rambunctious voice, one she probably used last when she was in a high school play. Sylvie has put me in charge of the barbeque. I try to think of this as an altruistic move, aimed at making me more comfortable. I keep busy, grilling meat and fish to everyone's specifications. Lily sails over every so often to kiss my cheek and pat my back approvingly.

"... and then the raft takes this big wave and we fly up in the air. And I'm trying to hang on," I hear Claude saying.

He is talking about a white-water rafting trip they all took one summer on the Gatineau River. He leaps out of his chair and starts demonstrating how Lily managed to save him after he went overboard.

"And here I am, twice her size, and she has me by the arm and she doesn't let go," he says.

Lily is tickling Andre, kissing his neck. They are laughing so hard that they don't hear the story.

*****

I have big plans for us today. A trip to the museum, followed by lunch at Lily's favourite restaurant, and maybe some shopping. I want to get her a piece of jewellery, something unique and beautiful to wear on our wedding day. But when I come downstairs for breakfast, Lily and Sylvie are already up and packing a lunch. Lily is dressed in lycra running pants and a T-shirt, clothes I've never seen before. She and Sylvie are laughing and talking when I come in. In French, of course. Lily is telling a story, her hands swirling madly, her face alive with enthusiasm. Sylvie is laughing when she sees me and looks a little guilty.

"Oh, good morning, darling," Lily says. "You're up!"

"Yeah, it looks like it," I say, trying to respond brightly but, instead, sounding peeved.

"Well, you're just in time," she says, giving me a neat, dry kiss just to the side of my mouth.

"We're making some sandwiches to take on our hike. What kind would you like?" she asks.

They are heading out of town for the day. No one had mentioned this to me.

"What about the museum? The exhibition is only on for three more days," I say, and even I am annoyed by the petulance in my voice.

"Baby," she says, indulgently, "we can do that on a rainy day. Not today, when the sun is shining!"

The preparations go on around me. A thermos is filled with lemonade from a glass pitcher in the fridge; oatmeal cookies are stacked into a plastic container. Andre is talking about his *lunettes*. Lily figures out that he wants to bring his binoculars on the hike, for watching birds and animals. They clatter upstairs to find them.

Sylvie and I sit in the kitchen at her big, old oak table, drinking strong coffee and eating pastries that Lily has bought at the bakery around the corner. Over the last few days, we've staked out some neutral territory, topics that we can discuss without any awkwardness. This morning, it's computers. We trade tips about upgrades and gadgets, good sites to visit on the Internet. She takes a long sip of coffee and looks away from me.

"You think she's fragile," Sylvie says. This is not a question.

"No," I say.

"Then why do you always want to take care of her?" she asks.

"I just think she needs reassurance sometimes."

"She's not a baby. She doesn't need to be coddled and fussed over," Sylvie says.

"What she needs is to feel secure," I say, putting my cup down on the table a little too forcefully. Some hot black coffee sloshes onto my hand.

"What she needs is to be treated like an adult," Sylvie says, and gets up from the table.

*****

I am the first to wake on the morning of the wedding. I sit in a wicker chair by the window and watch Lily. She is lying on her back, one leg hanging over the edge of the futon, the other stretched into the centre. Her mouth is slightly open, making her breath catch in her throat. A tiny snore escapes, then another one, louder this time, waking her. She shakes her head and touches her hair tentatively, then tousles it.

Yesterday, she came back to the house just in time for supper and modelled her new haircut. The long curtain of hair was gone, replaced by a cluster of short, red curls. Her face had changed completely. Her newly exposed jaw was strong, her eyes huge.

"Do you like?" she asked, twirling before us in the living room.

"It's great!" Sylvie offered immediately.

Lily turned to me, expectantly. So did Sylvie. I knew what I should have said. Instead, I muttered, "I loved your hair the way it was."

Now, with her hair tangled and her face soft from sleep, Lily looks like her old self, the one I wake up with every morning in St. John's.

"Good morning," I say. "Ready for the big day?"

She yawns and stretches for a few minutes before she sits up. Then she looks at me, concern creasing her face.

"Hal, darling, I've been thinking . . ."

My gut clenches. This is a feeling I have not experienced in a very long time. It's like driving your car along an icy road and feeling the wheels lose traction, knowing that you are about to leave the road and there is nothing you can do to stop what happens next.

"I mean, really, what's our big hurry?" Lily asks.

Family Business

My aunts all looked the same. Long noses, big horsey mouths, and a mop of curly hair that was always threatening to break free of a French roll. There were four of them, each born not a year after the last one. No wonder old Nan O'Neill's face was always screwed up, like she had sat on a tack or banged her bony shin off the gnarly leg of the dining room table.

Each of the aunts was named Mary something – Mary Margaret, Mary Elizabeth, Mary Patricia and Mary Agnes. But the O'Neills called them Peggy, Betty, Patsy and Aggie. After Nan had babies for four years running, she and Pop took a little rest. But by the time Aggie went to kindergarten at Mercy Convent, Nan finally came through with the boy child. They stuck him with the name John Francis William James Michael O'Neill, but they called him Mick. Most of the time, I called him Daddy, but sometimes I called him Mick, too, just for fun. It bugged my mother, though. She always told me not to be so "precious," so I would do it only when she wasn't in the room.

Nan O'Neill loved Mick more than life itself, I figured. He always got first pick of the chocolates when a new box of Pot of Gold was opened at Christmastime. Nan smiled at him from across the room, from her big velvet throne next to the fireplace, and she would say, "Mickey, give your mother a hand with these, will you, darling?" My mother usually left the room at this point, and if you were near her, you could hear her pretending to throw up. Mick would hop up from his chair and dart across the carpet to get at the chocolates. That's why there was never a maraschino cherry or a filbert cluster left for anyone else. But he made it up to me. There was always a full box of maraschino cherries in my stocking every year. I would eat them all before Christmas dinner, and sometimes I really did throw up. I just couldn't stop myself. It was a tradition.

Mick met my mother when he was at the university for a semester. She was taking History, Latin and Literature and making the honour roll. She was president of the Debating Society and played the violin in a quartet. Mick was there because Nan O'Neill said so. He was a boy, and it was his job to make the O'Neills proud by being the first in the family to walk across the stage in his cap and gown. But Mick spent a lot of time in the cafeteria, smoking cigarettes, drinking Pepsi and charming the girls, my mother says. He never went to classes. In fact, one of his professors posted a sign in the main lobby with Mick's picture on it and the words, "Have you seen this man?"

"That stupid old codger thought he was funny," Mick would grumble when my mother told the story.

"It *was* funny," my mother usually said. "We got a grand laugh out of it."

When my mother said "we," she meant her and Ted Hogan, her fiancé at the time. He was brilliant and witty, she said, with a little sniff in Mick's direction.

"Come on, Eleanor," my father said and chucked my mother under the chin when she talked about Ted. "Ted was a boring old fart who thought he was a big deal because he'd been in the war."

My mother always had the same response.

"Ted is a doctor and the president of the Knights of Columbus and a respected member of our community."

"And he'd put you to sleep in a second," said Mick, laughing and pretending to snore at the same time.

I liked to hear stories about how my parents got married and, of course, I got completely different versions from the two of them. I quizzed my father about it when we were alone in the car. He usually took me for a drive on Sundays if he got up before lunchtime. He would saunter into the living room with my coat flung over his arm and jingle his car keys at me.

"Care to go bouncing over the potholes, Miss O'Neill?" he would say, bowing grandly in my direction.

Our Sunday drives took us in one of two directions. Some days, it was time for a "bay run." My father called everything that existed outside the city limits of St. John's "the bay." We drove to Torbay or Middle Cove or Portugal Cove. That's often how I got my best stories. My father's tongue loosened up when he had a steering wheel in his hand. When Mick was feeling less ambitious, we stuck to the familiar streets of town. We would cruise out Monkstown Road and down over Prescott Street and make a few passes of Duckworth and Water Streets, waving to people out for their afternoon walks. Then, we retired to Willie's tavern for what my father called "afternoon refreshments."

Willie was not supposed to be open on Sundays, so we always went around to the back lane and sneaked in that way. It was a special arrangement for Willie's special friends. When we came in through the storage room, Willie always pretended to be surprised.

"Well, hello, old man! What brings you by on this fine Sunday afternoon? And who is the charming young lady with you?" he asked, as if Mick had never spent a whole Sunday afternoon there.

"William, it is a pleasure to see you," Mick said, shaking Willie's hand and slapping him on the shoulder. "This is my lovely daughter, Meg. We are just out for a Sunday drive."

"Is that so?" Willie said, and looked at me with a big smile. "Well, as you know, Mick, we're closed today. But can I offer you a beverage? On the house, of course."

He and my father exchanged a couple of exaggerated winks, and we took a seat at the bar. For me, a beverage meant a weird kind of lemonade that Jeanette, the barmaid, whipped up for me. And for Mick, it meant whiskey – neat. We usually sat there for a couple of hours, and I got some good stories out of my father this way. But it was hard to know if they were any bit true.

The way Mick told it, his romance with my mother was like a big Hollywood movie starring Rita Hayworth, shot in colour, with lots of dance scenes. Ted Hogan was out of town one weekend at a Catholic men's retreat, and Eleanor went to a dance at the parish hall with some of her girl-friends. They were chattering and giggling and casting long glances at the guys sitting nearby. But Eleanor just sat there in a dress as dark and dusky blue as a berry, with one long leg crossed over the other, and watched the action on the dance floor.

"The thing about your mother is that she loved to dance," Mick told me, as if he was letting out a dark secret. "But old Ted was a bumbler on the dance floor, so she never got a chance to strut her stuff."

On this particular night, Mick asked Eleanor to dance and twirled her around the floor, letting her dip and spin until she was dizzy. By the end of the evening, they were partners for an impromptu dance contest, which they won handily, Mick added with a wink.

"By then, she was hooked. There was no going back to Ted the Dead," he said, hopping out of his chair and walking around like a zombie. He did that all the time, but it still made me laugh until I snorted lemonade through my nose.

Eleanor broke off her engagement to Ted a few months later and started going out with Mick, a move that set the tongues a-wagging in town. People would look at them with narrowed eyes, as if they were hoping to peer into their heads and figure out what was going on between them. Their classmates came to the conclusion that Mick and Eleanor were a very odd match.

"Not that your mother cared," Mick told me, with a hint of pride. "She couldn't be bothered with what they all thought of her. Your mother was a bit of a mystery to the crowd at the university. They didn't know what to make of her."

There was no doubt that my mother was different from everyone else her age. For starters, she lived alone in a cottage on the top of the hill on Carpasian Road. She owned it outright. Her father had died when she was five and left the property to her. Her mother married again and had two little boys ("horrible little hellions," she called them) so Eleanor cleared out of there as soon as she was allowed. The cottage was a lovely spot with a fancy front room and a studio where she could practise the violin and set up an easel for her watercolours. She would heat up tins of soup for her supper and make toast in the little kitchen. And, in the afternoons, she would pour endless cups of tea for the girls, and they'd sit in the front room and talk and listen to the radio.

Eleanor's father also saw fit to leave her an inheritance. Nice of him, I figured. My mother wasn't rich, but she was "comfortable," as she called it. She had enough money to pay for her tuition at the university and for her violin lessons and art classes. And when she wanted a new piece of sheet music, she could just walk into Hutton's Music Store and tell the clerk to put it on her bill. And he always said, "Of course, Miss Tobin. That will be just fine." All the bills went to the lawyer, who paid them without comment every month. She did not have to explain herself to anyone.

"But everything changed when I married your father," my mother told me, and she sounded a bit sad then. I guess she really missed her music lessons.

Eleanor married Mick on a Sunday in August. A warm, silvery fog lingered over the wedding party for most of the afternoon, keeping the sun away. But it never rained, which was a blessing. As it was, Eleanor's fine hair was already frizzy from the damp air. Her friend Doris tried to control it with pins and sprays, but it floated over her head, puffy and cloud-like.

"Good thing you've got this hat," Doris said. "Otherwise, you'd look a fright."

"Aren't you a comfort!" Eleanor said, in her snippiest tone.

My mother didn't want to look like every other bride she knew, decked out in white gowns, with layers of white net shrouding their heads. Anyway, she said white did nothing for her fair skin and reddish hair. In the end, she wore a long dress of silvery blue with a wide-brimmed, floppy hat to match. The wedding ensemble came from the Model Shop downtown, and Eleanor thought it looked quite smart.

"Will there be any men at the reception?" Doris asked, while she fussed over Eleanor's hat.

"If there are, you'll have to fight Mick's sisters for them."

The wedding reception turned out to be quite the party. Mick and his friends kept things going for hours, drinking and singing, their arms thrown around one another's shoulders, their faces red and their eyes teary. Eleanor danced with Mick and his father, and each male guest in turn, whirling around the dance floor in her elegant gown, looking every bit the queen. Mick made several toasts to his new bride, the love of his life, the most gorgeous woman to ever set foot on the university campus. But each one made a little less sense than the last. It was almost three o'clock in the morning when Mick picked up Eleanor and swung her through the door of the cottage, knocking her head on the door frame.

After the wedding, Pop O'Neill decided it was time for Mick to be a man and earn a living for his family. It was finally time for him to join the family business.

"I will see you down at the store on Monday morning at eight o'clock," Pop told Mick.

But Nan intervened on Mick's behalf.

"Now, Francis, the boy has just gotten married. Give him a chance to get settled in," she said to Pop.

Pop tried to argue but it was useless. He gave in and said Mick could come in on Tuesday. Nan countered with a week from Monday and walked out of the room. The deal was done.

As the oldest, Aunt Peggy had been the first of the crowd to go to work at the family's clothing store. They sold overcoats and tweed jackets and salt and pepper caps to all the fine gentlemen in St. John's. After a couple of weeks on the job, it was clear to Pop that Peggy was a natural at the art of retail sales.

"It is a joy to see that girl sell a coat," he said, with genuine admiration. Pop was not too good with the customers himself. He was stiff and awkward and could never find much to say to people. So he had respect for someone who could cajole money out of people's wallets and make them feel happy about it at the same time.

But Peggy was modest about her success. She credited it to 40 per cent knowledge of the goods and 60 per cent knowledge of human nature.

"I just show the men what looks good on them, and if they look good, they feel good," she said, as if it was the easiest thing on earth.

On her thirty-fifth birthday, without a husband in sight, Peggy marked her seventeenth anniversary at the store. Under her direction, the O'Neills did well. Three years before, Pop bought the building next door and expanded the store, adding sections for children's and ladies' clothes. Pop decided to give Aunt Peggy a reward for her loyalty and the permanent toothy smile she had for the customers. It seemed that half of St John's went down to the harbour to await its arrival.

"It's a surprise," said Nan, when the aunts pressed her for details on the gift. She snapped her mouth shut like a change purse and said nothing else. A huge cargo ship was docked at one of the finger piers, and people were clustered on the wharf, looking up at the ship's deck in anticipation. I poked my mother every so often to suggest a possibility.

"Maybe it's a horse!" I speculated. "Or a husband!"

She looked down at me and gave me the darkest of her renowned dark looks.

"Really, Meg, is there any need to talk about your Aunt Peggy like that?" she asked, and I knew I was not expected to respond to that question.

My father was chatting with everything that moved on the dock. He buzzed around like his shoes were on fire. By that time, he had been working at the store for a while by then but it was not like anyone would have noticed, as my mother was fond of saying. Mick didn't actually spend a whole lot of time in the store. When I left for school in the mornings, he was still in bed. When I got home, he was rarely there. If he came home in time for supper, he would usually come in to the living room and listen to me play the piano for a few minutes. I tried to play something bright and upbeat to keep his attention, to keep him in the room. But I knew it hadn't worked when he got up and kissed me on the cheek, blowing his sweet whisky breath into my face. After that, it took only a few minutes before he and my mother were arguing in the kitchen.

"Look, something's coming off the boat," Aunt Aggie called out to the rest of the family.

I looked around for Mick to let him know the surprise was coming. But he was nowhere to be seen. Finally, I caught a glimpse of him standing off to the side, behind someone's truck. He was talking to Jeanette, the barmaid at Willie's tavern. She was eighteen, not old enough to work there, but she could handle the customers like nobody else, Willie said proudly, as if he had invented her himself. I liked Jeanette. She was kind of saucy and funny, and she swore more than most of the boys I knew. A rough bucket of bolts, my mother would have called her. When my father and Willie launched into baseball talk at the tavern, I asked Jeanette to teach me card games. She was a real pro. One time we were there, she showed me how to play Blackjack. She dealt like an expert, slapping the cards on the bar with authority. When I lost a hand, she laughed. She laughed a lot, with her mouth wide open and her head tossed back.

But Jeanette was not laughing that day at the waterfront. She was pointing at my father, her finger stabbing the air below his nose. Mick wore the strangest expression on his face. I slipped past my mother and sneaked through the crowd to get closer to the truck. Jeanette's voice bounced up and down, hitting high notes I had never heard from her before. By the time I got near the truck, I could hear that she was crying, sniffling as she kept on talking.

"I don't care what you tell Eleanor," I heard her say in a soft, muffled voice that I barely recognized.

"I'll work it out," Mick said, and he took her hand, patted it like it was a kitten or something.

"You better do something. I don't have much time," Jeanette said, and started fishing through her pockets for a tissue.

Behind me, people started clapping their hands. I looked up at the ship's crane hovering over the dock, a huge wooden box dangling from its claws. I looked back at my father and Jeanette. He was holding her arm just above the elbow. I stepped out from around the back of the truck, and Jeanette saw me first.

"Daddy, the surprise is coming off the boat right now," I said, and my voice was very calm.

Jeanette smiled at me and blew her nose. Mick let go of her arm and turned around.

"Right you are, darling," he said and started walking in my direction. He turned back to Jeanette. "I guess I'll see you later at Willie's."

The box was slowly moving towards the dock, inches at a time. I could see Aunt Peggy with her hands clutched together in front of her chest, as if she was about to sing with the Mercy Convent Glee Club. Pop was beaming at her. His face looked like it could bust open. When the box finally touched the ground, a couple of men rushed toward it with hammers in their hands. They started to pry the nails out and pull the end off the gigantic box. It was big enough for a half dozen people to stand up inside. Mick stood behind me, drumming his fingers on my shoulders in time to some tune he was whistling. My mother was a few feet away, watching us both.

The wooden square finally came free of the box, and the men pulled it away. Pop stepped forward and offered a hand to Peggy. They walked together and peered into the box. She turned around to the crowd and screeched, her hands over her mouth.

"It's a car! It's a brand-new Buick!" she said and did a little dance before she threw her arms around Pop and planted a big, wet kiss on his cheek.

The crowd was quiet as Aunt Peggy stood in front of the car, her mouth open and her hands fluttering. Then, my father started to clap, a loud, hollow sound echoing out of his cupped palms.

"Bravo, Peggy! No one deserves it as much as you," he called to her, and the rest of the people started applauding and whistling.

My mother looked at Mick curiously, as if she had never seen him before.

The next morning, my mother walked quietly into the living room and found me lying on my belly on the carpet, reading a book. I was supposed to be practising the piano, but she didn't seem to care. Instead, she perched on the piano bench and crossed her legs, one long, elegant leg over the other, the pointy toe of her shiny brown pump hovering near my face.

"How would you like to go on a trip to the Boston States? Just me and you! We'll get on the boat a week from Monday."

This got my attention. The Boston States were all we ever heard about from the aunts. Peggy and Patsy went there once to visit some of their girlfriends from Mercy Convent who had gone to get jobs. They lived in Cambridge and worked in the bank. Aunt Patsy gushed about the clothes they wore, smart suits nipped in at the waist and dresses splashed with polka dots, topped off with matching hats. Peggy talked mostly about the excellent business opportunities that existed there, especially in the gentlemen's apparel trade. But that just made Patsy giggle and snort.

"I don't think it was the apparel that caught her eye! I think it was all the fine gentlemen!" she said, one hand over her mouth to catch the laughter.

"That is not the case," Peggy shot back, all puffed up like a hen. "I am only interested in ways to improve the family business!"

Patsy said there were so many people from Newfoundland living in Cambridge that it almost felt like home. They even had dances especially for the expatriates. Ever since that trip, she had been trying to convince Pop that she should go down there and get a job, but he said he needed her at the store, too.

My mother had never been very keen on the idea of the Boston States. She always muttered that Patsy was just a bit too flighty for a woman her age.

"What is all the fuss about?" she'd ask, looking around for someone to give her an answer. "There is nothing in Boston that we couldn't have here in St. John's."

But on that day, she had a new attitude.

"Well, what do you think?" my mother said, and her foot started tapping on the hardwood floor.

"Sure," I said. "How long would we go for?"

"As long as we want."

Acknowledgments

The members of the Burning Rock Writing Collective in St. John's offered me insight and encouragement while I wrote these stories. Special thanks to Ramona Dearing, Larry Mathews, Lisa Moore and Claire Wilkshire. I also appreciate the support and advice of Ed Kavanagh and Helen Fogwill Porter, who have been wonderful writing coaches and mentors.

Thanks to my family and friends for reading, listening and cheering me on – especially Karen Ryan, Ken Ryan, Peggy Matchim, Anne-Marie McElrone, Susan Crocker, Michelle MacAfee, Lisa Porter and Maggie Keiley.

I would like to acknowledge financial support from the Newfoundland and Labrador Arts Council and the City of St. John's Arts Jury.

I am grateful to Dawn Roche and Dwayne LaFitte at Killick Press for gently shepherding this book through the publishing process. Finally, thanks to my editor Paul Bowdring for his sharp eye, patience and passion for the words.

Beth Ryan, St. John's
August 2003